FLIGHT 777
& GOLDEN FLIGHT
TO DUBAI

FLIGHT 777 & GOLDEN FLIGHT TO DUBAI

MVJAY

PARTRIDGE
A Penguin Random House Company

To order additional copies of this book, contact
Partridge India
000 800 10062 62
orders.india@partridgepublishing.com

www.partridgepublishing.com/india

[Two Stories at the price of one]

1. Presence of Aliens and UFOs has always fascinated the human race. The human race is keen in knowing whether outside human race there are any other race and if so whether it would get details about them. The myth, that disappearance of flight was due to Aliens leads to nice fiction.

2. In the second story the author has imagined how one would wish if luck always favoured him.

This Book contains two stories. One story is a fiction and another story is a short story. The two stories are packed as one book for the enjoyment of the reader.

STORY 1

FLIGHT 777

This story is a fiction based on some events that had happened in various times. This is totally an imaginative situation conceived to be presented as a fiction. The names, events and the situation etc are all imagination. The intention of the author is not to hurt the sentiments of any individual, organization or country in specific. Any resemblance of event if any visualized is only incidental. The author wants the reader to enjoy thoroughly the fiction.

LIM AND FAMILY

Pilot LIM KO KIN was driving along the Marine Drive area towards the national hospital. Marine drive National Hospital was one of the military hospitals with the sophisticated facilities for the Government staff. Lim KO Kin was born for a Japanese father and Korean mother. He works for the government aviation as a pilot. His wife Azhagi was bearing and expecting the child within another two months. Azhagi was born to a Sri Lankan and Indian and was working as ground staff of National Airlines. They both had to meet the doctor at the military hospital to discuss the procedure for admission and further follow up. They reached the National Hospital and parked the car. Lim was more tense which was very visible. His wife Azhagi was also a bit tense since doctors had given lots of test and were murmuring amongst them. She wanted to know whether there was any problem with the child that was growing inside her. They had to meet Dr. Linda who was well known amongst the fraternity for her excellent skills. She had seen lots of maternity cases and her patients knew pretty well that as long as her face wore smiling look there were no issues with their health. The moment there was slightest trace of worries on her face the patients also became nervous. Lim and Azhagi developed a feeling that Dr.Linda herself was foreseeing a difficulty. Such was the case with Azhagi.

The turn of Azhagi came and both Lim and Azhagi went inside. Doctor went through the routines and checked the reports. There was a slight trace of discomfort in the face of doctor. She just asked Azhagi whether she had any pain or discomfort. Azhagi replied negative. Doctor sent her out cleverly and retained Lim to discuss with him. Doctor started whispering in to ears of Lim. "Mr. Lim something looks different". Lim was trembling. He was very eager to see his ward soon. But the way Dr showed her expressions, he became panicky.

I am totally astonished said the doctor, "Till yesterday everything was normal. But I see some unusual movements. I want to have some tests. Anyhow, don't worry, I will take care". Lim was disturbed, came out and did not show his disappointment and informed Azhagi that some more routine test would be taken.

Dr.Linda updated her information day on day and always thought on lateral angles. She was more concerned about Azhagi's developments and she started her browsing and got deep into it. She had virtually cancelled all her appointments which were a rarity in her service. Even on acute ill health, she had attended to patients after taking proper protective steps, so that the patients did not get affected by her ill health. Today's situation was something very different.

Lim took his wife ceremoniously for the checkups and came back and waited for the results allowing Azhagi to rest in the general hall. He was getting more tensed since the results took time. He enquired at the counter and the clerk over the counter said that Dr.Linda herself had been following up the results and he would soon get a call. Lim sat in distress, since he did not find any abnormality on his wife. He started snoring slightly and a sudden call woke him up and it was his call and the reception wanted him to come to Dr. Linda's room. Lim held the hands of Azhagi firmly and took her inside the Doctor's cabin. By now, Dr Linda looked cool. She asked them to get admitted in the hospital that day itself and appointed some special doctors to attend to her.

Lim showed his Pass and took admission. Azhagi liked the spacious room. Doctors were very curious. They came one by one and it looked a bit unusual for both Lim and Azhagi about the seriousness that they were enquiring anxiously her feelings and health conditions. After sometime,

Dr Linda entered the room. Behind her, were a group of doctors seriously looking into the investigation reports. Linda took out all the reports and started analyzing it and she showed some items to her counterparts and asked them to monitor them. After all the doctors went out of the room, Azhagi called Lim and expressed a sigh of relief but nevertheless her face wore the anxiety. She whispered to Lim, "Lim! Everything is alright?"

Lim nodded his head and said "God is great!" Azhagi fell into sleep slowly and time passed on. Lim had just gone out of the room to relax and get some snacks and drinks for him. He was in deep contemplation as to the result and was more concerned about the child to be born. He was concerned about his wife too.

Lim was very much interested in aviation science since his child hood and liked to become a pilot. His father had got him lots of Chinese toys to play with. After finishing schooling he went for pilot training. He had gathered lots of equipments and simulators. He had good number of friends who were research scholars and he used his connection to deeply study the aviation field. He used to talk about all the machines available in the industry. He studied deeply the inner details of communication equipments and engineering designs of each and every model of planes. He gathered lots of information over a period and was called a master by his co pilots. He used to even guide his friends whenever they underwent troubles on board the plane. He had identified many possible troubles and designed trouble shooting for such troubles. He had recorded his experiences during various flights and he had lots of graphical presentation about the circumstances during such occasion. Those included the weather conditions, machine problems, surface level and outside the aircraft conditions etc. He had developed a great deal of passion towards his profession and he did it with zeal and passion. He had a good name with his superiors and was regarded as a through gentleman. He had a clean flight record and got few commendations too for having acted in extraordinary situations tactfully.

Azhagi on the other hand was a loveable girl. She enjoyed communicating to public and so chose the job in the airlines. She was a book lover and had very good collections. She was also very much interested in occult science which her forefathers from South India had bequeathed her, probably. She had also intuitive power and was sharp in her activities. She had good office records and had won best employee award from the air lines. She was loved by one and all. She always used to chide Lim that he was over engaging in officialdom at residence also and asked him to forget about aviation process and think of the family and its welfare. She was very much interested in Tamil literature and used to talk a lot on Vedic culture of India and more about "Adharvana Veda" which had lots of information on all scientific fields, more especially on space science and information on occult science. She used to meditate daily and had known yoga. She looked very bubbly and was liked by one and all in her surroundings.

Evening, Sun started fading and night entered. Lim had returned to the room and reached Azhagi and held hands firmly and looked into her eyes. He consoled her and expressed that everything would be okay and soon they would see the new baby. The medicines made Azhagi slightly drowsy and she started sleeping. Lim sat in the corner where he was allotted a place for rest. Lim was so tired that he fell into deep sleep and no amount of sound or tapping would wake him up.

As time was passing on, Azhagi started showing some symptoms of disturbance from sleep. She was moving this side and that side and she felt that someone was moving around her and just wanted to know whether it was Lim. She found Lim in deep sleep and just closed her eyes but again felt some meek sound and movement of some hazy figure moving around.

She opened her eyes fully and she could not decipher any particular figure but however wanted to caution Lim about someone else present in the room and gave a weak call to Lim. Lim was so deep in his sleep that he could not hear her call. Suddenly she felt that someone was touching her and she felt that she lost her voice fully. She could understand that she would not be able to make her voice louder. Suddenly the room got lit in yellowish orange colour over her and she could decipher three or four figures looking like near humans but with very big blue eyes and bigger head as would be for children with cerebral problems. The eyes were penetrative and they were sufficiently tall enough like American basket ball players. They were thin built but looked strong with tight muscles. The nose and mouth did not have any deep split like humans. Azhagi was startled since she had read books on Aliens and imagined Aliens in the same fashion. The figures formed some dimension near to human and stood around her. They were talking in very feeble voice which she could not hear however. Suddenly someone of them put his hand in front of her eyes and she felt dizzy and suddenly felt that something was inserted into her body. She tried to scream but no voice came out of her throat. She finally assumed that they were Aliens and were doing something with her baby. She felt some type of fluid got injected into her body but could not identify clearly where. She felt some pain but the hand over her eyes had made her to feel nothing. She was astonished about the happenings and she could hear a metallic voice telling into her ears that they were not humans and wanted that baby for them to accomplish some task. They cautioned her not to bother about the child and threatened her not to abandon the child lest she and her husband should lose their life. She felt dramatic and things went on and she could suddenly see the Aliens to sublime into air and the light had disappeared by then and was totally perplexed. Now she had an added worry about her husband. She wept in silence and continued her sleep silently.

When she woke up, she found Lim by her side with coffee in his hand. He helped her to do the morning routines and waited for the nurses and doctors for the routines. Nurses came and gave a towel bath and routine medicines. Team of doctors entered one by one and finished their routines. A lady doctor took her turn and on initial checking, her eye brows became tweaked. She ran mad and entered with Dr.Linda. Dr.Linda was also perplexed and she saw the face of Azhagi who was literally crying in silence. Dr.Linda then asked all except the lady Assistant Doctor, to get out of the room and started talking to Azhagi. She asked whether anyone else came inside the room and did anything. Azhagi was speechless and saw the lady Assistant Doctor. Taking a clue from Dr.Linda, that, lady Assistant Doctor went out of the room and Azhagi started crying again in silence holding firmly the hand of Dr. Linda. She explained everything she had noted in the night and Dr.Linda was deeply but calmly hearing the entire story and went into deep contemplation. She stoked Azhagi and consoled her and told her that the child would be born out and they would take care of her life and child's. She advised her not to share any information to any one on this event and said that she would be always in touch with her and her family as long as the child was with them. She had a lengthy discussion with Azhagi and made her to accept the fact that child to be born may not be like human also. But she gave enough strength to Azhagi so that she would survive her life. This message that Dr. Linda was staying with Azhagi for more time panicked Lim and more so the Chief of the hospital who came to know that lots of appointments of Dr. Linda got cancelled and he felt that something too serious should have happened and he peeped into the room of Azhagi when still Dr. Linda was talking to her. Dr. Linda explained the entire story and his face took the shape of tweak object. He was astonished with both the ladies that they had decided to face the situation and patted on the back of Azhagi and assured that the entire fraternity would come to her rescue.

They left the room after quite long time and Lim entered the room with sorrow. He asked Azhagi what had happened but could not understand anything since he had not expected such things and sat in silence in the corner given to him. He had requested for a sleeping pill from the doctor stating his status and went into slumber.

Sun set itself and Moon started arising. The hospital plunged into silence and the room became chiller. Suddenly Azhagi felt that again the room was lit with some orange light and she could now decipher the Aliens. They stood around her and the man who had talked to her initially looked into her eyes. He bent down and whispered into her ears and thanked for her decision to save the child and allow it to come into existence. He also assured that they would do something to make her happy after the baby was taken to her house. They left also a word of caution that no repeal of decision should be taken by them. They assured that they would be present when the baby would be born but informed that they would not be visible to anyone. They assured that they would save her life at any cost and assured her not to worry about her health and she would be back to normal human health. They assured that the child could be grown up like a normal child and can be educated like a normal child. The only difficulty would be his figure which might not be totally like a human. His capabilities would be of human and even more they said. Lying helpless, Azhagi got the message and went into sleep.

Dr. Linda cancelled all her weekend trips and she took up an appointment with the chief of hospital Dr.Rehman Malik who was a learned man. Patients would see him as a rationalist, atheist, scientist, philosopher and friend. He was a great thinker. Dr.Linda entered the room of Dr Rehman and started discussing the issue. She told the story in depth. She also informed him about her search in the internet about another case similar to that in US corner. That doctor has just shared some information similar to this but was not giving it in full. She gave the links of the US doctor and Dr. Rehman started surfing the net. He got the message and analyzed it. He was quick to identify the doctor as Dr.Franklin, a senior professor and practising physician globally known but due to age he retracted from the world news.

Dr.Rehman got him on phone and explained the situation and narrated the story of Azhagi. Dr. Franklin was sharing the humiliations he had met after revealing such instance in the net but however was ready to share lots of information after Dr. Rehman requested him persistently. He gave the information that the child born in US was not alive. He said that the lady was psychologically upset over the child's figure and died due to heart attack. The child was abandoned by the father and it was to be kept in hospital for some time. Dr. Franklin's story was not accepted by the US doctors. That patient had revealed same information like the one given by Azhagi but since the mother died, the child could not be reared by any one and just like that it died. He suggested that the Aliens might have also abandoned the child since the mother had died. He cautioned Dr Rehman to take care of the mother and ask her to be bold. He thought that if mother was alive, the Aliens would probably come to the rescue of the child. He revealed that the Aliens were doing this with something in mind. Dr Rehman heard all these things as a story. Being a practical person he would not believe many of the information, if told by a lay man. But since the voice on the other side was not less than a well known doctor he noted the information and shared the same with Dr. Linda. Finally, he told Linda that this child and mother should be saved at any cost so that they would be helpful in getting more information on this subject. They decided that the operation would be handled by only them along with one anesthesiologist who was a confidential man. Dr Rehman raised his doubt about informing the police and State about the strange event. Dr. Linda suggested that they would play down this story and silently do the delivery/operation and make the child go home and from there they would watch the child and monitor. They took oath not to speak about this out deliberately unless they had some sizeable information on the revelations of the Aliens. They also assured to themselves that they would attend to the child's issue at any cost and at any stage in its life and refrain from informing this event to State or police.

The day was fast approaching and every one the mother, father and two doctors with the anesthesiologist were expecting the event to happen. It was on 8th of March that the hospital heard the most shrilling voice of a bearing mother and the child was born. The child was having big blue eyes. The child looked like a child with blown up cerebrum. The child was heavier than a normal child. It was tall with long fingers and toes. The child opened its eyes and cried like human voice with coarse voice mingling. The doctors aptly handled the situation. The baby was identified as a boy and he showed normal health parameters for survival. However he could be only fed artificially with milk. There were lots of reasons for doing like this and doctors had taken the decision and advised Azhagi to accept their decision. Azhagi was upset terribly but could not do or say anything. Lim stayed with her for some days and started his routine. He requested Dr Rehman for assistance through some nurse which he obliged. Azhagi was preparing herself with the eventuality and after three months she started her official routine. She somehow warded off questions about her child stating some reason or other. Her colleagues also left her without pestering her expecting some problem with her child. However, they did not have any chance to know about the details of the child. The nurse appointed by the hospital unofficially, took charge of the child which showed tremendous growth and could understand as human. The nurse was a very experienced lady and she was a thorough professional. Dr.Rehman had requested her to keep confidentiality of the information. Evenings Azhagi would come home and spend her time with the child. She was wondering why this should happen to him.

Since the child was silent and not making any noise, she decided to name the child as "Nishubdh" The meaning was silence. She also liked the name. The child was lying on the ground silently observing the surrounding curiously.

After six months when Azhagi was washing the clothes and finishing day's routine, she could sense some movement within the house. Her husband had gone to office. She quickly ran towards the room where the Nishubdh was sleeping. She could not believe her eyes. She had seen the Aliens who had come to hospital. They had surrounded the child and were enjoying his features. They looked happy and they now and then touched the child. The child was also responding to their gestures. The child seemed to understand what they were saying. They took the child in turn and were saying something in its ears. They affectionately swayed their hands over the child and they could touch the thick nerves which were green in colour. Azhagi stood in silence watched the wonder taking place. The child, except head, was becoming near human. Head alone was slightly overblown and eyes looked different. The Aliens noticed her and came near her and hugged her with affection and put their hands on her head as blessings. Spell bound was Azhagi to see all these scenes. When she reached the child Nishubdh, he looked at her and it looked as though he acknowledged whatever had happened. Lim used to come then and there and he showed his affection to the child even though he would have been happy if only it had been a normal child. He used to bring lots of toys. Whenever he used to sit in the simulators or other computer machines the child would look on sitting on the hip of Azhagi and rejoice them.

The child was growing very fast than the humans. He could understand as human and Azhagi engaged a private tutor to teach him. He started moving out and other kids would see him with curiosity. Somehow he got settled with the children. Doctors Linda and Rehman used to visit her house often and check up the child. They were noting down lots of details whenever they came. The child started learning English, Malay and Tamil. The Aliens would visit the house whenever Lim was not there. They would have thought that he might not like their presence. They used to talk something to the child in its ears and the child also looked to acknowledge their teachings.

The child grew to the size of 6 foot by the age of 12. He used to sit with Lim and learn all the information about aviation science. He was able to negotiate the simulator with ease and grace. He understood all subjects easily and would look deep into each and every thing. Azhagi had developed doubts that the child is being educated by the Aliens to observe certain things. She felt that everything was out of control. She had a feeling that her worries have drastically reduced down to a great extent. However with great difficulty she tried to get admission to her son in a college.

The visits of Aliens increased. Azhagi noticed two prominent things with them. When they talked to her in her ears it was slow and metallic voice. She could see them as incapable of speaking as we would speak. Another thing which she noted was a startling and terrifying one. While playing on an occasion, Nishubdh had touched a bonding chemical in his hand while putting two broken toys together. The Aliens were present at that time watching him. To remove the paste from his hand Nishubdh wanted to dip his hand inside a kerosene bottle as his friends would do. He just reached the bottle and with an alarming sound one of the Aliens pounced on him and pulled him out of reach to kerosene. But before this could be done, some kerosene split on the forefingers of Nishubdh and that portion was vanishing into thin air. His finger got reduced by ½ inch. The Aliens were furious and pulled Nishubdh and gave some instructions in his ears. Nishubdh also to his astonishment saw his finger tips to melt like sugar in water. Azhagi was startled and she decided to keep Kerosene out of his reach.

One day Lim was in the cafeteria after finishing his flying hours. He was bored up and went to relax near the woods nearby the hotel where he was staying. There was no movement of persons and the entire area was tranquil. He went to a corner and started enjoying nature by taking deep breath. After sometime he could notice some movement around him and visibly he could not find any one. He turned around and found none. Suddenly from thin air, three or four men resembling his son but taller than his son, came and stood in front of him. They showed signs to invite him to still more lonely area. Then one of the persons talked into his ears. The leader said he had shown mercy to his child by bringing the child to near human form. He also said that the child would be left untouched if only Lim accepted their plan. Lim was hearing the metallic voice in silence and his face showed signs of misery and fear over the plan shared by the Alien. Then and there he wanted to intrude but the Alien did not allow him to talk at all. It looked as though they had brain washed Lim and Lim was just accepting their instructions. The Alien leader wanted Lim to arrange for Pass ports of four persons by crook or hook. He gave him a plan. The plan was that, on a particular day when Lim would be the main pilot, the four Aliens would fly with him since they wanted to enjoy flight travel. Lim asked them how they would produce a photograph for pass port. They said that they would change their true shape and come into human form to a greater extent and that would be sufficient for the pass port. Lim expressed his inability but the man was into his ears with sternness and Lim could only shake his head in affirmative.

Lim was upset about the happening. He wanted to share the information with his wife but was afraid she would decline the thing. He knew very well that she would not like to indulge in such activity. But he was afraid of his wife's life and more of his son. Just then his son had grown up and started moving with other boys. He did not want to lose him. He only worried that god was giving such tense moments to him in life. He thought life with Azhagi would be a bed of roses. But now it looks like a bed of thorns. Anyhow, he did not want to let down Azhagi. He came home and went straight into bed. Azhagi was a bit concerned about his behavior. She could understand that nothing was in her hand. Lim got up at mid night and searched his phone for some numbers. He could locate a travel agent who was known to him. Lim had helped him lot in his earlier years. He conveyed his idea of arranging passports to four people. His friend was perplexed and was wondering what happened to Lim. He knew Lim very well and knew that he was a genuine person. He said he would contact Lim after a day or two.

Lim got a call from his friend, the travel agent. The travel Agent reminded him of the call he had made. He wanted to know whether he requested for passport really or after taking drinks he had jovially asked for passports. Lim told him that he was under pressure and he and his family's safety stood in arranging for the passports. Lim also reminded of the earlier days' help he had done to him and requested that he should at any cost help Lim. The travel agent's end became suddenly silent and the phone was cut off. Lim was concerned about his silence and was worried about it a bit. He searched some other numbers and tried to fix a gang leader who had met Lim sometime back during one of his journey from Hongkong. He called him and requested him to arrange for passports. The fellow at the end identified quickly Lim and assured to revert back.

Lim was concerned about the passports but quickly returned to his office routines. He used to sit everyday with Nishubdh and work on simulator and communicating equipments. He was astonished the way Nishubdh had learnt things. They used to discuss lots of things about aviation. One day they were discussing about the speed of plane and minimum space required to land a plan. Lim was sharing his knowledge and was astonished when Nishubdh said that a plane can be halted in a short space provided there is another medium to accept its momentum. Lim did not clearly understand his son's point. He asked him to explain further. Nishubdh said that in god's particle experiments the speed was maneuvered by using some medium which can absorb the speed of particle. Similarly through a medium the speed can be brought drastically to zero. Lim was wondering about his revelations. He doubted it even though he believed that some super normal power was with his son.

Nishubdh showed extraordinary qualities in his studies and games. Due to his height he got admitted into the basket ball team. Once during a tournament he virtually flew from a long distance to take the ball and reversed it to his opponents net. All were astonished and he got the nick name Alien. Also when another player was obstructing him while shooting, he gave a mild jab and the opponent player strolled down. Nishubdh understood the situation and reduced his speed and run and moderately used them. He was a thrill to all his friends but his master was noticing him curiously and started studying him in depth.

It was a fine evening when Nishubdh and parents were relaxing at their home. Suddenly a big Rolls Royce car entered their campus and Dr.Rehman and Dr Linda came out of that. For a moment Lim and his wife were surprised but they managed. They invited the doctors inside their house. Dr Rehman wanted to see their son. Nishubdh came out and met the doctors. Doctors were surprised on seeing him. They asked Lim whether they are consulting any other doctor. Dr.Rehman was quick to notice the drastic change from non human form to human form in the child. Dr Linda touched the boy as though she was greeting and held his hand and flew her hand over his hand and was surprised to see the drastic change the boy had undergone. They asked her whether the family saw any movement of any other persons of abnormal or paranormal forces inside or outside their house. Both of them blinked and did not give any reply. Nishubdh was simply observing them. Dr Linda suggested to Lim that he could come with the child to the hospital and further have check up for his blood group and other factors if they were really interested. Dr.Rehman asked Lim whether his son developed any medical problem. After a brief stay, the doctors left the house and Nishubdh asked his parents who they were. They mildly avoided to answer and said they were friends from the physician family.

It was a pleasant morning when Lim got a call from his old friend travel agent asking him to contact for arranging for pass ports. Lim was happy. He took the details from the agent regarding his office and prepared for a travel towards the agent's office. The agent had asked him to arrange the photographs of the Aliens. Lim thought he had to wait for the arrival of the Aliens to get the photographs. He wanted to interact with his son and know what the Aliens had been communicating to him very often without his knowledge. Nishubdh was non committal. He requested Lim not to ask embarrassing questions and remained silent. Lim asked Nishubdh how he came to know about speed and its characters and details regarding stopping of moving items. Nishubdh involuntarily expressed that the Aliens used to teach him lots of things then and there when they visited the house. He also revealed shocking news that on some occasions they would not be visible to human eyes. He also startled with some other information that the original four people were not repeatedly coming and some others were also coming to meet him. Since all of them were looking same, probably Lim and his wife might not have understood who they were. He said he did not know when they would come.

Day by day mystery was developing and it became quite interesting for Lim to know about the Aliens. What was perturbing his mind was why these Aliens were trying to interact with his family like this. He took interest in the blogs revealing details of Aliens and UFOs and started gathering information. He was more curious about the change of form and figure by the Aliens and his son too from that of sub human form to human form. He developed some paranormal feelings about the Aliens. He did not take into account the request of the Aliens to travel by flight for enjoying the ride. His mind was saying that some other plan might be with them. He started analyzing the different angles of their request. The first idea that came to his mind was of hijacking the flight. If it was so where they would land the flight?. Wherever they landed the flight that would be identified by the satellites or radars. If the idea was to hijack then what was the motive. Were they going to learn about the plane? When they could develop much more superior things than human why should they highjack a plane? If there idea was to take the plan to another destination away from earth then where they would go for fuel. Whether they would use nuclear fuel and if so how they would load it within the aircraft. All these questions pondered over his mind. He was expecting the Aliens to react to him again in arranging for a travel. An occasion came when the Aliens had entered the house and the leader sat with Lim while others were interacting with his son. The leader asked Lim whether he considered getting passports for them and arranging to take them for a flight experience. Lim tried to avoid, but the leader stressed and nearly threatened that he should do it at any cost. Then Lim came out with a feeble request for their photographs to arrange for passports. To his astonishments, the leader asked the team members to come forward and each one was photographed by Nishubdh and Nishubdh was photographed by his father with the special camera brought by them. When the photo was given for print at a local studio,

Lim was surprised to see that there were near human faces for all the team members including his son. Lim got the photos and returned home. He was in deep contemplation as to whether he should go to police or somehow manage by himself. He was also perturbed by the visit of doctors.

Lim contacted the travel agent and handed over the photos. He told him to keep everything in strict confidence. The agent looked at him curiously and said as long as there was no problem for him everything was OK for him. The agent assured to arrange for the passports from some of the underworld gangs and give a call. Lim looked at him with gratitude. He was wondering how the underworld gang would manipulate such passports. Days went by and there was no reply from the agent. Lim had a positive hope that he would get the passports soon. His worry now was not the passports but how to manipulate other formalities to take them on board the flight.

Doctor Linda and Rehman were closeted for quite long time. They had put the other Doctor Franklin on conference and the discussion was on. Dr.Franklin commented that there were all possibilities that the Aliens were visiting the house of Lim. He was also critical that they might have made some manipulations on the child. His way of arguments made Dr.Rehman and Linda to think that they had come on a mission and they had chosen Lim and Azhagi couple to get their things executed. They were thinking of discussing the issue with police but more worried about the formalities. They were not also certain to provide authentic details to the police in case they go for investigation. They decided to remain silent to avoid further confusions. But one thing was certain that they had got some intriguing message about all the happenings.

Lim's phone was continuously ringing. He had returned from the flight schedule and was asleep. Suddenly he woke up and took up the phone. The person at the other end was none other than the Agent. He informed Lim that the passports had been made ready and wanted him to take delivery of the same immediately to avoid any problem for him. Lim affirmed him and proceeded immediately to his place to take delivery of the passports. He reached the agent's office, who took him inside an interior room wherein he handed over the passports to him and took his money. He finally cautioned him not to reveal his name in case of any problem. Lim's hand was heavy with the passports and his heart too. He had never done such thing in life but his son and wife's life was foremost important to him. He thought everything would be settled easily. He never would have imagined what would happen on the day of their travel.

CARD

China **Aliens** Research Department **(CARD)** was brisk with activities with scientist going here and there. There was an announcement regarding an emergency meeting to be held on that day. All were attentive in listening to the message. The meeting was regarding a discussion on the latest activities of Aliens. Each department head was expected to attend the meeting with particulars required. The entire centre became more active and all departments started gathering latest information to be submitted to the sponsors of the meeting. The International department was active in screening data and background of many foreigners meticulously. There were 5 important names finalized for submission to sponsors. The list contained names of 4 persons of Chinese origin and one person of Indian origin. The Five scientists were doing research in the field of Aliens. The one from India, by name Shanthi was a specialist in Adharvana Veda and was more informative on subject Aliens. The particulars about them were made into dossiers and kept ready for presentation.

The meeting started sharp and the senior heads of departments had gathered in the hall. The hall was silent with each one readying for the seminar. The head of CARD (China Aliens Research Department) started the meeting. He brought to the notice of all concerned that lots of developments have taken place in the field and many people have started seeing Aliens or their vehicles in remote corners of various countries. He wanted them to take clues from all available sources and wanted the participation of all concerned.

The various departmental heads shared with the leader, all the developments that had been made. Some had come prepared with presentations on the scientific developments in identifying the Aliens and their travel equipment. Some had come with the sketches of the Alien figures and some had brought the news collected by the American Doctor Franklin with finer messages. There was a team which had developed the study of the speed of the Alien's vehicles, Size of the Aliens, Language of the Aliens and the Communication Patterns of the Aliens.

It was the turn of International department which had produced the five names claiming that these five people had done extensive research on the subject. It also said that Four Chinese were staying in the Pak-Afghan border in the hilly regions where any external approach by any country or military was ruled out. It contended that the four member Chinese Gang might itself hold captive one or two Aliens under them. It had also contended that the team might get help from the Chinese Top bosses themselves. The lone Indian was a specialist in Indian Vedic studies especially in Adharvana Veda which dealt with all scientific fields in which developments had taken place today. The Ancient Indians had not recorded their knowledge in print form and mostly everything they possessed was given in the form of Gurukula meaning teacher passing on the knowledge to the student directly. Very few had recorded their knowledge in Palm leaves which were guarded by few in remote places of South India and Nepal. The Indian Scholar was a lady who was well versed with both physical science and occult science. She had guided these Chinese to a great extent often on the subject Aliens. She had met the scientist while travelling and that friendship had brought her with the Chinese gang in the work of Aliens.

All the departmental heads had concluded their submissions and the leader took all the materials and with his deputy he left the room. Every one stood as a mark of respect and the meeting came to a conclusion. The leader with his deputy then set for the next internal meeting. The meeting discussed for a seminar to be arranged soon on the subject. It was decided to hold the seminar as international seminar and invite for scientist across the Globe was planned. CARD had created link with scientists world over and had shared data with various countries in the field of Aliens. This time it was expected to have a good participation from worldwide. There was a report of latest developments in the small committee. It was reported that the CARD was able to capture two Aliens alive and have been conducting enquiry and various tests and analysis on them. It was reported that it was very difficult to communicate to the Aliens and feeding them was also not possible. Their food pattern was not known. The Aliens had metallic voice and CARD men were unable to understand what was being communicated. The Aliens looked very adamant and were seen rotating their eyes in all directions. CARD men had communicated that it might be dangerous to keep them for long time also since they might send data through their body sensors to their natives about activities of CARD also. At this juncture only it was contemplated to bring in the Indian Scientist cum Adharvana Veda specialist. The Indian was expected to use his personal skills in communicating to the Aliens through the psychic methods known to her. The Chinese gang which itself was believed to hold one or two Aliens as captives was requested to assist CARD. It was also reported that there may be attempt of the Aliens to relieve their colleagues from the hold of CARD. It was ordered to maintain strict vigilance over security measures and if required Army's support to be taken. The capturing of the Aliens did not make the CARD very happy because they also expected a retaliating effect from that event. What they would have appreciated was that this capture should have taken place after they had understood about some more information on the Aliens. Nevertheless it was decided to proceed further without any let up in any matter and at any stage. The date and time of the international seminar was decided as 9th March. There was lot of expectation from the four Chinese researchers and the Indian. The entire machinery across the country was activated for participation and all establishments were informed to share any information about UFOs they had come across, any information about Para normal activities, any information on movement of specific objects in the space etc. CARD was determined to go ahead with all possible efforts to know about the Aliens' movements across the globe. The leader made frantic efforts to reach out to the US doctor who was supposed to have some important information on this topic. A special envoy was arranged by him to reach out to Dr.Franklin to share vital information. The envoy was instructed strictly not to divulge any information to anyone on this. The envoy also made all out efforts to reach Dr. Franklin. He was discussing about the seminar and extended the invitation on behalf of the CARD and requested Dr.Franklin to attend the seminar. Doctor refused to comment at that moment but however gave some closed cover probably containing about some information about the Aliens. Doctor communicated to the CARD agent that those information are very confidential and should not be shared with all except the leader. The persistent efforts by the agent to make the Doctor to attend the seminar ended as futile effort. He quoted his old age and his shunning away the scientific community for quite some time as reason for not attending the conference. However, he extended positive help to share any information in future if he would get some. The agent took the gathered information and returned to CARD centre and shared it with the leader. The leader's face got lit up on seeing the information Dr had shared through the documents. He passed it on along with other dossiers through the agent to the next deputy.

Four Member Team

The Chinese team working from an island near Malaysia had been in this field for past several years. It was believed to have support from the Chinese government. They had a meeting point near PAK-Afghan border where they used to conduct lots of activities in testing various articles supposed to have been left by Aliens. Their hide out was kept as secret. They used to do their research activities in the island near Malaysia but their data was safeguarded at the place in Pak Afghan border. These scientists had advanced to a great extent in learning about the Aliens. The team had sophisticated equipments and machinery to conduct the experiments. They had developed super telescopic instruments which could be used to see the fast moving objects. The team had made a tiny helicopter model flying machine with which they used to travel to different isolated areas. The team always moved in a group of two or four and used to carry sufficient self defense equipments and some special radar to notice any special movement in the sky. The Pak-Afghan area is the one which they loved since there were many bunker type of natural hideouts which were not visible easily to others including flying aircrafts or satellites. While they were rounding around the Afghan border area they found these hideouts and they identified a den like place for conducting their secret activities. They had developed the area with sophisticated equipments slowly and made a laboratory type of accommodation. While they were involved in some research activities they had noticed two non human figures on the hilly area without any motion. They should have been toppled out of some flying object. For the Chinese, who were working on the Aliens this was a surprise. When the scientists approached those two figures they did not show any resistance. The Chinese dragged them into their den but did not know whether they were alive or need any first aid. They had collected some information about the Aliens but it was not sufficient to treat them in case of distress. At that time only they thought of the Indian Ms Shanthi who was well versed in the field of Aliens. They had come into contact with an Indian who was also a scientist but with a back ground of Vedic knowledge. The Indian had shared lots of information with these Chinese scientists regarding the Aliens and this had brought these five people together in the research of Aliens. The Chinese finally contacted the Indian and told her about the two unmoving Aliens accommodated in their den. They wanted her guidance in treating the Aliens. For that the Indian had told that the Aliens could not be treated with human medicines or techniques. She advised that they would conserve energy by themselves over a period of time. She advised them to keep the Aliens inside a captivity surrounded by Kerosene so that they would not escape from there. She also said that if this was not done, the Aliens on getting up after sometime would be very much destructive and destroy their lab and themselves. The Chinese had followed the advice meticulously and put the captured Aliens inside kerosene chamber. The Aliens had by themselves recovered and remained mute without making any attempt to escape. The Chinese were wondering about the advice of the Indian and proceed with their research work. They found to feed the Aliens or interact with the Alien. The place was so deep that any Alien attempt to reach out to these captured Aliens might not have been possible since the den was isolated. Even the Chinese had difficulties in sensing signals through their own equipment when they were within the den.

In this context only the Chinese scientists had been trying to meet the Indian in person. While they were on that contemplation only, they got the invite from the CARD. They wanted to contact the Indian and decided to take along with them for the seminar. They had just discussed about it and the leader of the team decided to send a message to Ms Shanthi, the Indian. Their idea was to meet the Indian and take her to the hide out and show her the Aliens under captivity. They hoped that the Indian would be able to throw more information on seeing the Alien in person. The Chinese firmly believed that the Indian had the capability to communicate with the Aliens. The short association with the Indian had enlightened the Chinese on her capabilities and they always enjoyed any discussion with the Indian.

MS SHANTHI,
THE INDIAN SCIENTIST

Ms Shanthi was an Indian freelance scientist from South India. She had educated from the good institutions in India and abroad and had learnt lots about the Vedic literature from their great grandparents. She had an in-depth knowledge in Adharvana Veda. She had developed this interest because any latest scientific development had always a mention in the Vedic scripts. She used to lament about the non digitizing data by the ancient Hindus. She had special capability to get into a "trans". When she gets into that transition stage she would talk in different languages. She would be able to interact with anyone. She had met the Chinese at one such occasion when she started talking in Chinese. Actually she did not know Chinese language initially. When she became friends with the Chinese gang she thought that she should learn Chinese and she did so. She was able to fluently talk in Chinese language. She used to share lots of information on Aliens with the Chinese. She had told them that the information should be used for constructive purposes only and not for any destructive purposes. She was astonished when she received a call from the Chinese about the Alien like figures identified by them. She had assured them that she would meet them and along with them she would meet the Aliens and try to talk to them using her "trans" method so that she would guide the Chinese for a possible treatment to the Aliens. She had communicated this to the Chinese and at that juncture only she got the invite from the CARD. She was surprised to have received an invite from the CARD and was wondering how those people would have got her details. Any how she was very happy to have received the invitation and she wanted to just to talk to their Chinese counterparts in the island. She had prepared lots of information dossiers to be shared with the Chinese team. She was eager to see the Aliens in captivity and this invitation gave a chance to meet the Aliens. She wanted to talk to the Chinese about the invitation too.

It was evening when she got a call from the senior scientist from the island. The gentleman was talking about the invitation from CARD and wanted to discuss some information with her. She also confirmed that she too got the invitation and said that she would come to meet them at a common point. She conveyed that she had gathered lots of information on the Aliens and wanted to share the same with them. She informed that she would meet them in Malaysia in the first week of March and discuss in detail before leaving for CARD seminar. She also showed her interest to meet the Aliens held captive and her interest to interact with them.

After making the dossiers ready, she sat on meditation and got secluded. She went into deep meditation and when she got up she was not happy and felt that whether she should proceed with the trip to Malaysia. She had a Guru and mentor for her and she went and met him. The Guru also went into deep meditation and opened his eyes and with a smile said, "Do not worry my dear child. Everything is for good only. You need not cancel the trip and you can proceed and you are going to win laurels." Her Guru was a very capable person. He only had taught lots of techniques and tantric tactics and clues to Shanthi. His Guru used to always insist that these tantric tactics should be used for self defense and should not be used to destroy another person. Her Guru had also taught her high moral values. As per Guru she came to understand various States of living things in the Universe numbering 14 which God had created and one such living State is the Alien State. She regarded her Guru's preaching very much and that is why thought that they would meet the Aliens and try to do some help for them to return to their own state.

AEM

AEM is short form of **Aliens' Earth Mission**. It was a team formed by the Aliens to study the earth and its contents. The AEM was more concerned about the invasion of outer space by the people from the earth. AEM had been working for last 40 years visibly to our eyes and had been rounding the earth to know the possible information. It had sent lots of UFOs which were seen by the people on the earth. It had created a team and a lab to process the information gained through the AEM team. Out of the set up they had teams studying the capabilities of the people on the earth in general engineering, space science, atomic science, aero science etc. It had studied the maximum speed attainable by an earthen machine. It had studied about the communication system of people of earth. It had studied the scientific developments done at various countries on earth. It was also responsible for swallowing two flights by an UFO without leaving a clue whether the plane was hijacked or crashed. It had taken captive of some important scientists who have been working on space science.

AEM had well equipped labs and excellent research centers on outer space especially to read about the humans from the earth. They were well ahead of technology than the humans. The worrying factor for them was the competing speed with which the human race was growing in science and technology. The AEM was most worried when their leadership informed them that few of the Aliens had been captured by humans and were safely held as captive and their whereabouts not known. The Aliens had a system of reflecting a sonic ray from their dress to identify their location. This time they could not be located after being missed. The AEM was given the task of relieving those Aliens captured by the human. The AEM had sent missions over the earth to locate the missing Aliens but could not locate. They had developed doubts that the human race had learnt some technology to hide the Aliens from other Aliens and this was the intriguing factor for the AEM. The AEM team was waiting for information on the missing Aliens. Days had gone but no clues were received by the AEM team.

The AEM team decided to venture into forming a Alien-human figure and train it with both the Alien state of technology and the earth's state of technology and science so that they can use that Alien–human in their favour to study more about the human technology and science and also to identify the missing Aliens. The team wanted to select the area wherein the child would be born. The concern of the team was that the people at the place selected should be able to observe this human-Alien in the right spirit and grow the child. They should not kill the child or take the child into custody into a lab. The team wanted the child to be born in a family that would cherish the child even though it does not have full human form and try to grow it up to some age so that the team of Aliens could interact with the child. The team would give the Alien technology and with the mix of human and Alien technology, the child could be used to know more about the human technological development and to identify the missing Alien on earth. The problem faced by the Alien team was that of the shape of the Alien child. The Alien child would be different without a full human form. The Alien quality genes should be imbibed in the womb of the mother with knack and the child born would have blend of both human and Alien qualities. The team selected United States as the Country where in the hospital would be identified and the doctor attending to the women would be identified. After identifying both, the Aliens would make the child born as Alien- human child and force the mother to accept the child. The family would be given all assistance to grow up the child. The Alien team would also try to bring a near human form for the child so that the child would be accepted in the human society as a disabled child. The human might identify the deformity as cerebral malfunction. The child might have bigger head than normal child with bigger eyes with blue colour. The voice might be coarse and the figure would be skinny. The nose and the mouth of the child would tweak to give an ugly look but humans would soon tolerate the child and allow it to grow along with them. With this in mind, the team of Aliens selected the place, hospital and the lady who was expected to give delivery. The hospital was headed by Dr Franklin who was well experienced and talented. During the late weeks of pregnancy the identified lady got admitted for delivery. On a fine late evening, after the doctors had done the normal routine, the Alien team entered the room wherein the lady got admitted. The room was lit with yellowish orange colour and the lady felt that someone was present in the room. The Aliens had surrounded the lady and soon she became senseless. The Alien injected some fluid into her body. The lady resisted the move even though she had lost her senses. The Aliens informed her that the baby that would be born would be having features of Alien and threatened her to accept the baby and grow it. They vanished into the air and the lady woke up with a jolt. She thought it was a dream and left it like that. Doctors doing routine checkups found some abnormality but let it casually. When the child was born, it was a terrible experience for the hospital authorities and the mother. Dr Franklin was terribly upset with this. He chided his juniors for missing to note the changes in the patient's reports.

The mother of the child was totally upset. She mentally became ill. She felt very much that she should not have taken light the event that happened on the evening when Aliens had invaded her room. She thought that she should have shared information with the doctors. Repeatedly thinking on this, the mother suddenly developed chest pain. Doctors immediately rushed to her help. Any amount of treatment could not bring her to normalcy. Since she was under continuous monitoring the Aliens could not also enter the room for any help. The vigilant doctors could not help the lady from a massive heart attack and she died. The child was left alone. The hospital tried to take care of the child to some extent. Since the mother had died and father was not forthcoming to adopt the child, the hospital clinically kept the child alive. Feeding was a problem and normal medical attendance could not save the child. Dr Franklin was too saddened. He had read lots of articles on Aliens and paranormal living beings. This was a different experience for him. He thought if only mother had taken the event too lightly, lots of improvement could have been done. He also had a feeling that the Aliens might themselves have come forward to help the child and mother. But everything looked like a fiction to him. He noted the entire event meticulously and reported it in a medical congress wherein he was mocked at, ridiculed and chided by his fraternity. It was a bad experience for both the doctor and the Aliens.

Days moved on and suddenly the earth sensors of the AEM got activated and it was a message that some Alien is sending information from the earth for the use of AEM. The AEM started recovering the message from the super electronic server sent by the Aliens from earth. The message read about the global meet of the scientist all over the world to discuss about the Aliens. The message gave out the details of the event, persons participating and there were highlights in the message which was mentioning about the four Chinese and One Indian. The message gave a detailed plan of these five people in particular and had sent a request to take on this mission. The message also emphasized that if the seminar was allowed it would pave the way for information gathering by the human race about the Aliens. The AEM was advised to take a serious note of the event and arrange the necessary things. The message was immediately sent to their leadership who in turn got closeted on to a meeting.

THE AEM WAY

AEM leadership planned to prepare and send a team of Aliens to earth to locate the flight by which these 5 people will be travelling. Since Aliens had received the details about the travel plan from the Aliens of earth they tried to identify the flight by which these five people namely 4 Chinese and One Indian would be flying. The selected team was advised to make a human-Alien form of a person somehow who can handle both space and earth requirements of travel. The team was advised to know about the operating techniques of the latest super aircraft by which these 5 earthen lives will be travelling. AEM also advised for producing a big balloon which could be floated over the sea in a strategic location which would not be located by the earth's satellites. The balloon would be having an inside set up with gaseous liquid medium which would be able to stop the speeding aircraft and halt it within 1000 metres range. The size of the balloon would be made in such a way that it would look like a flame when seen from the ground and it would be construed like a forest fire and get unnoticed. The balloon would also have all the facilities to hold the aircraft in safe position and shift itself to Indonesian-Vietnam area where it would get set into thick forest. Inside the forest, arrangements would be made by the Aliens already on earth to safeguard the balloon and make necessary arrangement required for the aircraft and its occupants.

A detailed plan was drawn to send a team to the earth to identify the flight, persons to give birth an Alien-human boy, to make the pilot to come into the hold of the Aliens by coercion, to take fake travel documents to fly by the same flight in which the 5 member gang was flying to attend the seminar, to take the flight away from the watching radars and equipments, to divert the aircraft in two or three directions to avoid the satellites easily, to bring the aircraft to such level that it would come in front of the balloon which would swallow the aircraft and fly to the destination already planned. The plan given to the pilot was to keep the flight away from the radars, deactivate the batteries of the black box which would send signals in case the flight is searched. The AEM chalked out a plan which should be implemented when the aircraft was stopped inside the balloon. A detailed plan was prepared by the AEM and given to the team of Aliens who were selected to attack the flight.

The moment the flight was swallowed by the plane it would be stopped in order to avoid waste of fuel. The team inside the cabin would come out and spray a special liquid through ducts which would make all the people inside the aircraft to fall asleep. They could be kept sleeping for the next several hours. The Alien team would identify the five member gang and take them into custody. In case of any eventuality they were not taken as captive, all out efforts to kill the five member gang should be done. The gang would be taken into custody positively. Once the gang was taken into custody, two of the Chinese team would be taken in a small Alien vehicle and with the Chinese team the captive Aliens would be located and picked up by the small Alien vehicle. It would then return to the Balloon. The plane would be brought out of the balloon and kept in the dense forest. The flight would be loaded with fuel and power and its communication systems would be activated after it takes off from the forest. It would get in touch with the Vietnamese bases and land up there and start demanding the release of Aliens held captive by the Chinese. A small Alien vehicle would be made available to pick the Aliens released by the CARD. Once the Aliens were taken back from the CARD, the flight would be released without the five member gang and Alien-Human boy. The Alien team, released Aliens, Five member gang and the Alien-Human boy would be taken back to the Alien state. The plan was chalked out clearly and passed on to the team for implementation. With that plan only the team from the Alien state reached earth and got in touch with the pilot Lim. They made Azhagi to give birth to a Human-Alien son and made Lim to accept the plan of the Aliens.

IMPLEMENTATION OF AEM PLAN

Now the real implementation plan had to be worked. The Aliens had come to closeted meeting with Lim and Nishubdh. They explained the process to Lim. They made Lim to arrange for tickets for them. They decided the method of entry into Airport and getting the seats allotted in the aircraft. In case of any detection by the immigration authorities, how to escape from the scene was also contemplated. Lim would be taking some liquid spray provided by Aliens to make the passengers to sleep in his personal kit. The liquid would be supplied by the Alien team at the appropriate time. While flying Lim would ask the co-pilot to get out to the cockpit somehow and make the way for the Aliens and his son. The flight would be in touch with the control room and suddenly reduce the height and deactivate the communicating systems. The flight would be diverting in two or three directions across Indian Ocean, starting from Andamans to Australia and would turn towards Indonesia and fly low and come in front of the balloon kept by the Aliens to trap the flight. By the time the flight takes the route to Indonesia, Nishubdh would be in-charge of the flight and he would drive the aircraft inside the balloon with accuracy so that the flight lands smoothly. The Alien team would spray the fluid through the air circulation system and all the passengers would be made to sleep. The Alien team then would start searching for the gang of five and identify them and take them to a corner spot. Once the gang was taken into custody, two of the Chinese team would be taken in a small Alien vehicle and with the Chinese team the captive Aliens would be located and picked up by the small Alien vehicle. It would then return to the Balloon. The Balloon would then take off to an undisclosed destination and land near Indonesian-Vietnam border among the thick forest as discussed where they would not be easily detected by the radars. The plane would be brought out of the balloon and kept in the dense forest. The flight would be loaded with power and its communication systems would be activated after it takes off from the forest. It would get in touch with the Vietnamese bases and land up there and start demanding the release of Aliens held captive by the Chinese. A small Alien vehicle would be made available to pick the Aliens released by the CARD. Once the Aliens were taken back from the CARD, the flight would be released without the five member gang and Alien-Human boy. The Alien team, released Aliens, Five member gang and the Alien-Human boy would be taken back to the Alien state. Lim and his son were hearing the plan with their mouth opened. They could not believe what was going on. They were more worried about the trouble to erupt on that day.

In particular, Lim was more worried by the fact that the Aliens would take his son Nishubdh along with them. He wanted to make a request to the Aliens whether they would leave his son along with him. The Aliens did not give a positive nod but did not negative his request also. He thought that they were afraid whether he would cooperate or not. He expressed to them that he would extend his fullest cooperation to them but insisted that Nishubdh was released with him. He had developed a deep bondage with him. Nishubdh was also noticing this and he also wanted to negotiate with the Alien team to get released from them.

Days passed on. Everyone was eagerly expecting the date of travel. The Aliens had selected the March 8th flight since they had messages that it would be the date on which the gang of 4 and Indian would be travelling to China to attend the seminar. Lim made the tickets for the four Aliens and his son in the same flight. He had prepared his tour luggage in which the liquid to be sprayed inside the aircraft was kept. While packing, he saw few spray bottles. He thought of some idea and placed them inside the luggage. Suddenly his eyes went towards a gallon of liquid written as kerosene. He filled one bottle with kerosene with the sprayer. He took that also inside his luggage and covered everything so that nothing left any doubt in the minds of the checking authorities. He was sure, being the pilot, his luggage would escape scan and he would be able to take these materials inside the cabin. His next duty was to select a co-pilot of his choice who would help him and understand him in case of dire necessity.

While the Aliens had their own plan of execution, Lim thought he would plan his action. He wanted to share his feelings with his son. He thought he would talk in detail about all these things with his son and his wife. He told them that he would like to share his mind with them on the ongoing developments. One night Lim sat with his wife and son. He told them that he regarded them as his wealth and he did not want any loss of wealth. He told his son the entire episode before his birth, how doctors helped him and how the Aliens reached him and further story. He told his son that he wanted him to be a human, a real human in all respects. He said Human was the only race which knew the word pardon. Patience, tolerance and forbearance were the qualities of human life. Above all forgiving the offender was the basic human great quality. Nishubdh was listening to all these things. He asked why the Chinese should take the Aliens as captive which had resulted in their invasion into human territory. He was of strong opinion that the Aliens captured should be handed over to the Aliens state back. He said when research could be done on the Aliens, taking them into captivity did not look human. He said if that was approved then Aliens' view would also have to be approved.

Azhagi intervened and pacified both. She said that for research sake whatever the Chinese team had done might not be right. But they would have done it for the betterment of the humanity. They would have thought whether any mileage could be taken out of their inventions and that was why the Aliens would have been held captive. Nishubdh did not accept that point at all. He convinced her finally that they would compromise on a situation where the Aliens would be released to the Alien State and the humans would be released to the Human state. He was of the opinion that research could be on the life and style of Aliens and their properties but not by capturing them. Lim was happy that he could get his son to a compromising stand. He thought that he would still persuade him and make him understand the human stand and to go along with it. Lim was planning further strategy that might be required to handle the situation smoothly. He mentally prepared for any eventuality in case the problem started at the immigration level itself. He carefully selected his co-pilot who was his best friend and had been co flying very often and understands Lim very well. Generally Lim was very cordial with all other staff that they would oblige him at any point. Lim arranged for the tickets for the Aliens and his son too and wanted to hold a meeting to share the ways and means to enter into airport without any hurdles and into the aircraft then.

The Aliens had come to the dining table at Mr. Lim's. They showed signs of relief since Lim had done all the required things for the travel. They sharply watched Lim saying the methods of reaching the airport and then entering the airport. They also took clues to follow the instructions of Lim for a smooth entry into aircraft. The leader of the Aliens wanted to confirm with Lim whether the liquid he had given to him had been packed inside his package. After confirming the details the leader set into a meeting with someone in remote area. He was talking in a metallic low voice to his counterpart. Probably he was giving the plan of action for the day. He wanted Nishubdh to stay with him when he conversed. Nishubdh looked to have understood the conversation. Lim was keenly observing the conversation but could not understand what was being transpired. After sometime they all dispersed and Lim called his son and locked into his bedroom. Lim asked Nishubdh to explain what they were talking. With reluctance Nishubdh shared what they were talking. Lim was startled on hearing the entire talk.

Aliens had decided to float the big balloon as earlier discussed and if by chance any rebellion action came from the inmates of the aircraft then the entire balloon would squeeze itself and suffocate the humans but make the Aliens escape. They also decided the ways to treat Nishubdh in different situations. That was the concern for Lim. Though with reluctance Nishubdh explained this he convinced his dad that everything would take place smoothly and the humans would be safely returned to their race without any damage. The trio father, mother and son were a bit weird and that they saw themselves in a strange situation. The team of Lim's family and the Aliens were set for the date of travel on March 8th.

Number 8: A Potential and Fatalistic Number

March 8Th was a great day. Number eight according to Chaldean, Greek and Hindu numerology was a symbol of fate and fate driven acts. Number eight on zodiac symbol Pisces always played a crucial role of the Saturn God who is otherwise called the King of Fate. All who were bound to be airborne by the flight were readying themselves. On the previous day, the Indian, Shanthi got up early and went to her Guru and took his blessings. His Guru gave her certain clues on the Tantric Veda. He was seeing her with full concentration with his face stern. He got a sacred thread and tied on her left hand and put his hand on her forehead at the centre of eyebrows and pressed it deeply. Then he opened his eyes and blessed her and bade her good bye. She took the flight to Malaysia to catch the flight 777. She had arrived early and wanted to convey the same to her Guru who in turn gave some more messages which she noted with curiosity and reverence. There was a chanting specially given to her that would make herself disappear from the scene and hang around on air without being noticed by any one. She was wondering why such chanting was given to her by her Guru. She got the chant by heart and wanted to talk to the Chinese and to ascertain their travel plans. They were too eager to talk to her and wanted to share some information with her and got the address of stay of Shanthi.

The Chinese had prepared well for the travel day. They had on the previous day packed their research papers. They exchanged information amongst them quickly and took some papers which they wanted to share with Shanthi, the Indian. The papers contained the reaction of the Aliens to various sounds. The Chinese had wanted to share with Shanthi, the reaction of the Aliens to the rhythmic sound of OM. Shanthi had given a chanting consisting of sound 'OM' to the Chinese while teaching them some of the yoga exercises. They used to utter the chants when they were practicing yoga. While doing so their observation was that the Aliens reacted sharply to the vibrations made by these chants and looked disturbed. The Aliens looked to have lost their concentration when they heard the sound of chant. The Chinese as planned met Shanthi and chatted for quite some time and shared the information they wanted to share. They also wanted Shanthi to meet the Aliens under captivity. That time it struck Shanthi that the Chant Mantra given by her Guru contained lots of the words OM. She was just thinking of the same to correlate it to the news given by the Chinese. They bade good bye to each other and dispersed for the day. Shanthi decided to meet the Aliens after they returned from the Seminar. The next day being March 8th was travel date to China to attend the conference.

The Aliens, Lim and his son, the Chinese gang, the lone Indian and other 200 odd travelers arrived at the airport at Malaysia. The airport was brisk with activities. Each one was tense with their travel documents at the immigration centre and one by one got their boarding passes. When the turn of the Aliens came suddenly the quickly moving queue stopped and started dormant. The officials at the immigration counter repeatedly looked into the passport and with an air of doubt were stamping the travel documents of the Aliens and Nishubdh. The police officials also looked curious on to them and very slowly allowed them all inside the arena. The Chinese had come with their travel documents and entered into the boarding hall. The Indian along with some other passengers also reached the boarding hall.

Lim had taken the baggage along with him through the special entry. Suddenly one of the Checking officials stopped Lim and rattled him whether he would check the baggage. Lim was startled initially but somehow managed and gave a crack jawed laugh at the checking official. The official was making more mocking and said he would like to check him thoroughly on his person. Lim stayed cool. Then the checking officials moved away stating that he did it for fun and said that he would not disbelieve a sincere servant like Lim. He cleared the way for the baggage of Lim and Lim took a deep breath as a sigh of relief.

The counter lady was announcing the flight departure of flight 777 repeatedly and asked all the passengers to get ready for boarding. She was communicating to the passengers waiting in the boarding hall that they would be readying themselves for the flight in next few minutes. When everyone was on the lounge of the boarding arena, Shanthi could look directly into the eyes of the Aliens and something struck her. She initially withdrew her eyes from them, but again stared at them. She could understand something different. The Aliens who had also seen the Indian quickly left the place sensing they are being looked into by a person who looked to possess super normal powers of human being. Suddenly there was a call for the passenger by name Nishubdh. The caller over the mike wanted Nishubdh to come to immigration department immediately. Lim was hearing this incidentally and he also joined Nishubdh fearing something wrong. The verifying official looked into the documents and saw Lim by his side. Lim gave a crack jawed laugh and said it was his son and he was accompanying him in his flight. The verifying official curiously looked at them and cleared the documents. With lots of tension and stress all of them started entering the aircraft. Shanthi was first among them to board the plane. She identified her place and sat followed by the Chinese. The Aliens and Nishubdh entered the plane and the moment they entered into the cabin, the sharp eyes of Shanthi fell on them. Her eyes scanned them virtually and it was felt by the Aliens too. She could not remove her eyes from those since she felt something abnormal and her inner conscience said something to her. The

Aliens quickly moved on to their seat which was conveniently located at the front. They were able to easily get up and move here and there, it was nearer to cockpit. Lim got into the plane through the special entry along with his baggage and split his luggage so as to easily identify the items at the time of necessity. The flight was getting ready to fly. The ground clearance was obtained and the plane started moving across the stationed planes and crossing the luggage carriers and steered towards the take off path. The ground clearance put the flight on to its path and the messages were exchanged between the control room and the cockpit.

The last words from the cockpit were "Good night Flight seven seven seven", changing the account from the previous "All right, good night.".

10:25:53 Flight 777 Delivery Flight 777 Good Morning

10:26:02 ATC Flight 777 Standby and xxxxx Six is cleared to xxxxxxxxxxxxxxxxxxxxxxx Departure six thousand feet xxxxx two one zero six

10:26:19 ATC ... Flight 777 request level

10:26:21 Flight 777 Flight 777 we are ready requesting flight level three five zero to Beijing

10:26:39 ATC Flight 777 is cleared to Beijing via PIBOS A Departure Six Thousand Feet xxxxx two one five seven

10:26:45 Flight 777 Beijing PIBOS A Six Thousand xxxxxx two one five seven, Flight 777 Thank You

10:26:53 ATC Flight 777 Welcome over to ground

10:26:55 Flight 777 Good Day

xxxxxx GROUND

10:27:27 Flight 777 Ground Flight 777 Good morning xxxxxx One Requesting push and start

10:27: 34 ATC Flight xxxxxx Ground Morning Push back and start approved Runway 32 Right Exit via xxxxxx 4.

10:27:40 Flight 777 Push back and start approved 32 Right Exit via xxxxx 4 POB229 XxXxXxXxXx…..

10:27:45 ATC Copied

10:32:13 Flight 777 Flight 777 request taxi.

10:32:26 ATC Flight 777…….. standard route. Hold short xxxx

10:32:30 Flight 777 Ground, Flight 777. You are unreadable. Xxxx to holding point xxx 11 Runway 32 Right via standard route. Hold short xxxx.

10:32:42 Flight 777 xxx 11 Standard route Hold short xxxx Flight 777.

10:35:53 ATC Flight 777 Tower

10:36:19 ATC (garbled) … Tower … (garbled)

Flight 777 Flight Thank you

XXXXX TOWER

10:36:30 Flight 777 Tower Flight 777 Morning

10:36:38 Flight 777 good morning. XXXX Tower. Holding point….10 32 Right

10:36:50 Flight 777 xxxx 10 Flight 777

10:38 :43 ATC 777 line up 32 Right xxx 10. Flight 777 Line up 32 Right xxx 10 Flight 777

10:40:38 ATC 777 32 Right Cleared for take-off. Good night.

Flight 777 32 Right Cleared for take-off Flight 777. Thank you Bye.

XXXXX APPROACH

10:42:05 Flight 777 Departure Flight Seven Seven Seven

10:42:10 ATC Flight 777 xxx xxxx xxxx identified. Climb flight level one eight zero cancel SID turn right direct to XXXXX

101:42:48 Flight 777 Okay level one eight zero direct IGARI XXXXX one err Seven Seven Seven

10:42:52 ATC XXXX Seven Seven Seven contact XXXX Radar One Three Two Six good night

Flight 777 Night One Three Two Six XXXX Flight 777

XXXX RADAR (AREA)

10:46:51 Flight 777 XXXX Control Flight seven seven seven.

10:46:51 ATC Flight Seven SevenSeven XXXX radar Good Morning climb flight level two five zero

10:46:54 Flight 777 Morning level two five zero Flight 777

10:50:06 ATC Flight 777 climb flight level three five zero

10:50:09 Flight 777 Flight level three five zero Flight 777

11:01:14 Flight 777 maintaining level three five zero

11:01:19 ATC Flight 777

11:07:55 Flight SevenSeven Seven maintaining level three five zero

11:08:00 ATC Flight 777

11:19:24 ATC Flight 777 contact Hi Cho Mi 120 decimal 9 Good Night

01:19:29 Flight 777 Good Night Flight 777

The Plane zoomed into air and started floating. The usual ceremonial warnings and instructions were all given by the girls of the airlines. Next warm up drinks and chocolates along with ear plugs were supplied. Passengers started settling themselves with their hand luggage and the plane started moving. Lim was into full swing action. He just took the aircraft above the ground level and started floating. The Aliens quickly one by one moved. One of the Aliens took the bottle from Lim's luggage and took the special liquid and sprayed into the air circulating mechanism and the liquid vaporized into the cabin. All the passengers started feeling dizzy and went into deep slumber. The four Aliens then entered the cockpit along with Nishubdh and Lim gave way for Nishubdh to steer the plane. The Aliens stood nearby Nishubdh and asked him to fly in to lower altitudes so that the radars did not identify the aircraft. They asked Nishubdh to take diversions. The transponders which made the plane visible to radars were shut off by the team. The diversions were still caught on military radars. The plane transshipped into other side of the land area and started flowing towards Indian Ocean. In front of the plane was a vast stretch of blue waters sprawling across vast area. The flight was flying low so that no radars or equipment could trace it. The loss of signal made the ground controlling units alarming. Quick messages were exchanged and countries all over the world were alerted about the loss of signal. The intelligence agencies all over the world woke up and the real search started as for as the human race was concerned.

Nishubdh had replaced Lim. He was at ease at the cockpit. He steadied the speed of the plane. He was flying low over the sea in Indian Ocean. Suddenly in front of him stood a big yellow mass, should be the balloon as referred by the Aliens. The other Aliens gave Nishubdh guidance and the mouth of the balloon could be located. Nishubdh noted the mouth of the balloon to open up sufficiently to hold the aircraft. He could not guess the length of the balloon but was confident that it would contain the aircraft easily. The mouth of the balloon opened up fully and Nishubdh slowly and steadily let the plane into it. At the first instant he could not see the entire inside of the balloon fully but when he entered the balloon he could identify it as a runway. He reduced the speed of the plane slightly and could feel that the plane was floating through some medium and to his astonishment could find that the plane came to a halt without any rough landing or jolt. The flight 777 got inside the balloon and the mouth of the balloon got closed. This scene was sighted by a villager as a burning ball of flame and he spread a message that he saw some glowing object.

The yellow balloon started to take off with the aircraft inside it. The balloon steadily rose upwards vertically with the entire load and started drifting from the Indian Ocean towards Indonesian Vietnam border. The balloon skipped all radars both civilian and military and reached the hilly hide out of Vietnam-Indonesia border and landed smoothly over a vast area. The way the balloon travelled showed the engineering marvel of the Aliens. There was no jolt or jump and the landing was again so smooth. There was no heavy sound even after the landing. All the inmates of the plane were asleep and would not have felt such transshipment. The gaseous liquid that was spread by the Aliens had good effect on the inmates except one person Shanthi who looked like sleeping but in fact was awake. She had used her capabilities of yoga and Vedic breathing procedures and had survived the sleep. She did not show it outside. But she could not understand what was happening. She could only see some diversions of the plane and landing on some smooth area. She was also wondering to note that the flight after landing was still flying to some destination. She did not show herself to be awake. She wanted to observe as many matter as possible.

After landing, the team of Aliens tried to identify the four Chinese. Shanthi using her tantric skills changed the facial look of the Chinese and

51

the Chinese looked like a combination of Chinese and American face. The Aliens struggled to identify the Chinese. They had not understood that the Indian had done the magic on them. The Aliens were patient enough to identify the Chinese without disturbing others. The trick was there for few hours only. The faces of Chinese came back to normal form and thus were identified by the Alien gang. They also identified Shanthi. They further gave an injection to the Chinese and pulled them into the last corner of the aircraft. Temporarily, they did not do anything to this Indian and the team reached cockpit. In the cockpit they gave the job of patrolling to Lim and Nishubdh and through the cockpit they got down inside the balloon and swayed through the medium to the corner of the balloon where they had a small Alien vehicle with all latest navigational equipments to handle on earth orbit. Two of the Aliens took the small Alien Vehicle and came near cockpit. The other two Aliens reached the corner of the plane and reached the Chinese. By that time the Chinese were woken up by the Aliens, but were so weak that they did not resist anything. The Aliens locked their hands with some type of handcuff and took them towards the cockpit and reached the waiting Alien Vehicle. It was like a compact helicopter.

The Alien took Nishubdh with them as a translator. They conveyed to the Chinese to disclose the place where they had hidden the Aliens they had captured. Nishubdh translated the Alien language to English and conveyed the same to the Chinese. The Chinese were mum initially, but when the Alien took out an injection and injected a dose, the Chinese cried heavily and they could not bear the pain that the medicine had given. They had their head spit into pieces and through some small equipment they were increasing the blood pressure of the Chinese. The Chinese were in unbearable pain. They finally revealed that the Aliens were kept captive in a hideout in China under the guard of CARD and explained what *CARD* was.

The Alien team arranged for a communication system using the aircraft and contacted the CARD leader through the captivated Chinese. The Chinese accepted to explain to the CARD agency about their plight and assured to get information about the area where the Aliens had been kept captive. The Chinese talked to CARD agency and explained in detail the story so far from their departure. The CARD agency swiftly pressed into service some supersonic flying system to reach out to the Aliens vehicle. Meanwhile, sensing some action like that by the Chinese, the Aliens had given a cover to their vehicle which would make it not detectable to human eyes or equipments. The CARD agency finally decided to release the Aliens and assured the Chinese who were under captivation to come with the Aliens to pick them up. Chinese passed on the message to the Aliens. The leader of the Aliens made a head counts of the missing Aliens and had a doubt that the Chinese themselves might have some Aliens under their captivity. They further tortured the Chinese and pressed for more information and the Chinese accepted that they had also taken two Aliens under their captivity. The team started. The small Alien vehicle took off speedily. The ride was so smooth. The vehicle was evading all the radars and satellites. The navigation system was superb and the Chinese wondered about it. They guided the Aliens how to reach the place where they had kept the Aliens under arrest. With the sophisticated navigation system they reached near the captive place. The equipment inside the vehicle started showing symptoms of the presence of other Aliens but the signals were weak. The vehicle reached Afghan border where the Chinese showed them the hide out where they had kept the Aliens. The Chinese had held the Aliens captive and kept them in a big glass vessel which had an outer cover. Kerosene was filled in the gap between the two cylindrical shapes of the container. The Chinese had known that the Aliens would resist any move to come into contact with the liquid like kerosene. However they had not known what would be the effect of kerosene on the Aliens. They did not venture to test it also. The Aliens had taken the Chinese inside the den area and keeping one Chinese as captive they got the Aliens released from the captivity. One of the Aliens thoroughly checked the Alien and after thorough checking he put his hand on his head and pressed it heavily on the captive Alien. There was a blue ray of light passing from the new Alien to the captive Alien. It took some time for the Alien to come to normalcy. He showed some symptoms of shamefulness and came to normalcy soon. The Alien vehicle took those Aliens who had been kept as captive and returned to the balloon.

The Chinese were wondering about the transporting system of the Aliens. They were wondering about the silent and fast moving vehicle and wondered about its accuracy and swiftness. The Alien vehicle reached the balloon and landed near the cockpit and they took the Chinese to their seats. The Aliens were handed over to the leader and he did some tests on them for any microphone or sensor system and after confirming that nothing of that sort existed he took them into the gang and narrated the entire episode to them. The desperate captivated Aliens patiently heard the story and in turn they told how erroneously they got caught inside the Chinese trap. Whatever they had observed in the laboratories of the Chinese they had shared with the leader and remained silent. They also reminded about other missing Aliens and suggested that they might have also been captured by the Chinese only. The Chinese upon hearing from the scientist had sent some spying vehicles to locate the balloon. The Chinese spying vehicles could not locate the balloon and returned to their bases without identifying the Alien vehicle.

The news about the mysterious disappearance of the flight 777 was flashed out by the news agencies worldwide. Everyone was expecting some hijacking event or extraordinary sabotage by terror group including suicide attempt by the pilot. Some experts had predicted that the flight have plunged into sea due to some extraordinary circumstances and thus would have gone away from the radar. The various news agencies gathered report about the disappearance and were telecasting the event. The search for the plane was over the Gulf of Thailand, South China Sea and Strait of Malacca wherein the plane's communication system contacted or the military radar spotted. Experts had analyzed the contact between satellite and plane and finally concluded that it might have crashed over South Indian Ocean. The government agencies of flight 777 were persuaded by other Nations world wide to seek the help of experts to identify the reasons for the mysterious disappearance.

The Police took the details of all the travellers and found that four passports have been faked. They got into the CCTV clippings and identified the seat numbers on which the four people had travelled. The police also had gone through the track record of the pilot who had extraordinary good report of flying. Even though there were some wrong apprehensions about his aviation science knowledge, the police did not magnify the same. The police went into the history of the pilot and co pilot and traced the family traits of the pilot. They came into contact with Azhagi and had a detailed enquiry with her. They repeatedly asked her about her son and his nature and they started collecting information about his capability from the surrounding neighbours and from his friends.

Azhagi had informed about the special child and told about the doctors who had attended on her while the pregnancy was on. Police reached Dr Linda and her boss and Dr Franklin. They collected all the details about the child but could not make any headway to link it to the case of disappearing flight. Azhagi was tense with the police enquiry. She could not reveal the entire thing. She was also more concerned about the news paper news and television channels news that the flight might have landed up into the sea. She thought some untoward incident should have happened and thus the disaster would have happened. The police reached the passport agency which had prepared the fake passport and arrested the owner. It was revealed that the passports were taken on the prompting by the pilot. Somehow the agencies were unable to reveal the name of Lim. Police were clueless.

After the Disappearance

Search operations were initiated worldwide. Initially the search operations were over Malaysia, Thailand and then to Andaman Nicobar area and then to Deep South Indian coast and then towards the New Zealand and Australian sea waters. Worldwide protests from various countries started coming up. The Chinese authorities had requested for the participation of the entire nations' forces to trace the plane. The plane was searched on all the big seas. The search was encouraged initially by the floating objects found in the seas by India, Australia and New Zealand. The American agencies lent its help to search the flight. The group 5 nations had gathered the information about the five scientists flying by the plane and came closeted for a special meeting in knowing the reason for the hijack. It was decided to employ all resources to identify the reason for the disappearance and to locate the flight's parts and black box. Sometimes some positive information about the black box would come but soon the information would die down stating that it was not correct. Lots of scientific theories were floated to explain the process of disappearance.

Mr. Kumar was an Indian who worked on numerology. He used his occult power with the skill on numerology. Numerology was his hobby. Many people contacted him for knowing their future. Many Politicians and Leaders used to come to him for getting advice on various matters. It was on March 8th that an officer from a bank who was a neighbor to Kumar contacted him about a missing colleague from his own bank. Kumar took the date of birth of the missing person and calculated something and told his friend that the person who was born on 4th had quarreled with his wife and gone to a far off place and would return on

17th of March without fail. The officer friend who had come to Kumar immediately showed some of the photographs of both husband and wife and asked a pertinent question. "Sir in the photograph they pose very close and there does not seem any difference of opinion between them" Kumar was stubborn in his reply and said that he did not want to comment on anything but said the gentleman would return by March 17th. Next was the turn of a Politician. The Politician had asked whether he should contest elections this year. Kumar nodded his head positively and told him to file his nomination papers. This gentleman was one who was discouraged last time by many soothsayers, numerologists and Astrologists, when he wanted to contest in elections. Kumar was the lone person who gave him a positive reply. At that time his Political leader had not assured him a seat even. But later the leader gave him a seat and the Politician had to take on a communist leader as an opponent. He was not sure whether he would win. It was Mr. Kumar who saw the results of the leader in TV and communicated his victory news. Anticipating defeat the leader had gone underground. Like this Kumar had many predictions done to his friends and relatives.

The Bank gentleman who happened to be Kumar's neighbor again re-entered Kumar's residence with the news of the missing plane. Kumar went into Trans and said that on March 22nd the plane would return without much damage to it or its passengers. His neighbor was spell bound and was astonished also. He had earlier brought some of his friends to meet Mr. Kumar. He had known Kumar's success rate in his predictions.

It was on the same day that the relative of the Indian passenger Shanthi met her Guruji seeking blessings and information on the missing flight. Guruji was in deep contemplation and opened his eyes and coolly told the relative of Ms Shanthi that she would return definitely but not immediately. He also assured that nothing would happen to the plane and everyone would mostly return safely. He expressed that the flight was indeed hijacked but not by human but by Aliens. This news spread across the world and many laughed at his expressions. But the family members of the Indian did believe in Guruji's words. Guruji smilingly said that everything would end smoothly and without any damage all would return including the aircraft. This view was very seriously analyzed and followed up worldwide by many agencies and countries. It went as a viral message worldwide.

The CARD agency also got the information about the missing flight 777. It was eagerly expecting the Chinese and Indian for the conference. But they never thought that they would get a message like this. They were perplexed to know that there might be some hijacking event or the flight would have submerged into water. The leaders did not want to take any unauthorized messages but however wanted to continue with the seminar. They wanted to discuss whatever that would have happened till the time they boarded the flight and till the time flight disappeared. CARD had expected that there may be some attempts to intercept the flight to capture the Chinese by some terrorist organization. The expectation was that such group would demand heavy pay out and release the Chinese against such funding. But they never thought that there would be some other way of knowing them as missing. But they did not want to confirm anything unless they hear or see things with their own eyes.

The CARD agency also pressed into service many sleuths to follow up this event and also follow up people related with this event as reported in TV channels or Radio channels. There were delegations made to Malaysia, India and US. The doctors Linda, Rehman Malik and Franklin were all targets for watching by the Chinese agency. The agency also had plans to approach Azhagi to know more information.

The CARD agency would not have thought that the Aliens captured by the four Chinese gang had been released by the Alien team. They wanted to contact them but never knew the method of doing so. They had some strong feeling that something should have gone wrong somewhere which might have given clue to the Aliens that humans had held Aliens as captives. The enquiry from Azhagi, Dr Linda, Dr.Rehman Malik and Dr Franklin suggested that some Alien team had intruded into earth and are on search mission for their associates. The missing plane mystery, targeting the flight in which the Chinese were travelling and the Chinese gang holding some Alien as captive all these information made the CARD to rethink on the subject and they closeted for a meeting to discuss the various aspects of the missing plane. They were eagerly expecting the Chinese to contact them through some source.

THE FINAL STAGE

The Aliens decided to go further into action. The balloon prepared itself to release the aircraft out of the balloon. The other side of the balloon was opened up and Nishubdh was given the pilot's seat. The balloon ignited its system and the balloon rose up and distanced itself in such a way that the aircraft could take off. Lim was surprised to see the extended and flattened balloon which gave a long runway for the aircraft to take off and land at the terrain. The aircraft was specially fuelled with some special liquid which got mixed with the aviation fluid. The Aliens had mastered the technology behind the aircraft. The communications equipments were initially jammed for non detection. The balloon got ready with the part of the team of Aliens and it got lifted to a distant place so as to make the aircraft to takeoff and open its communication systems for contacting the nearest airports or military base. The balloon was insulated for non detection of the balloon. The job of handling aircraft was given back to Nishubdh and Lim. The Aliens had taken three Chinese with them into the balloon and left one Chinese and Indian to contact the Chinese authorities for releasing the Aliens with the CARD. Lim reactivated the communication systems and switched the engine. He tried to contact the nearest radar and the one he could get was that of the Vietnamese base. He swiftly narrated the story of the hijack and wanted to land there. He clearly told the base commanders that the aircraft was heavily loaded with explosives and tightly guarded by the terrorist who had passports from Malaysia.

Mr. Lim continued his conversation and somehow convinced the authorities of the base to permit him to land there. He assured he had gauged the terrorists and found them sensible and assured that once their demands are met out, the plane would be released. He pleaded help and said that the lives of 200 odd passengers were at stake. He somehow took permission to land there. The message that the flight 777 had been hijacked itself was welcome news for the Nations worldwide. Every nation which had possibility to join search operations extended their cooperation. This message gave them the hope that the passengers were alive. But no clue about the terrorist or their demands was made known to them. The military base made arrangements for the flight 777 to land at their naval base. The flight was surrounded by the commandos and all service operations like supplying food water etc was kept ready. Lim negotiated with the commander and took the essentials like water food etc.

The news spread like a wild fire. The news that the flight 777 was still in physical form and no untoward thing happened to it was good news to the world over. The news that spread from the base sent alert signals from all countries across the globe for any possible mission to rescue the plane. Top leaders of big countries got closeted for discussion for possible next action by them if required. Chinese authorities immediately flashed the news that the flight 777 was well intact and all the passengers were safe and no accident as contemplated had happened. Everywhere prayer meetings were convened. The Big 5 nations got into some meeting to ascertain what would have happened to the flight 777 for these many days. Everyone was surprised to know how the flight could spend nearly two weeks in darkness and escaping the radars and now land up in a military base.

The news also got spread across India. Suddenly Mr. Kumar became point of discussion by many because he only predicted through numerology that the flight would come out on 22nd of March. Everyone started talking about him. Much of media hype was created about his foretelling. On the other side of the peninsula, Guruji was also talked about. The disciples of the Guruji thronged at his Ashram and congratulated him for predicting the correct position. Shanthi's family members were very happy to know that she was alive and all others were also alive. People thronged on both these gentlemen, namely Kumar and Guruji to know further information about the event. Some channels narrated the story of top ten missing flights in which one flight was supposed to be swallowed by an UFO. Many linked the information with that of Guruji's message that the Aliens might have hijacked the flight. All said and done it was pleasant day for one and all over the world that a disaster had not happened.

The gaseous liquid which had kept the passengers asleep loosened its clutches on them and passengers came back to normalcy. They were blinking to find the environment quite calm and some sort of seriousness was observed. They did not have the information that they had been hijacked. They were given clear instruction by Lim and co about what they should do and not do. The Aliens had changed their appearance back to the original position as in the pass port. The lone Chinese was given strict instructions not to act smart. Shanthi had understood the situation. She could identify the Aliens with her special powers. The Chinese man was allowed to sit by her side and he narrated the entire story. The Alien leader through Lim started the negotiation. He confirmed to the base people that the plane was loaded with inflammable liquid and no attempt should be made to strike them. He said he meant business and assured to release all the passengers once their demand was met out. The base commander wanted to know what their request was. He was startled to know that the some paranormal had only taken possession of the aircraft. He decided this based on the metallic and undecipherable voice of the Aliens. He also came to this conclusion from the demand they made that the captive by the Chinese should be released. They did not reveal the names of the captives and the place from where they are to be released which amused the commander. He had known through the military intelligence that CARD was dealing with paranormal human beings and Aliens. He started the negotiation. He wanted to know who should be contacted and where the captives should be brought in case it was accepted. The leader of the Aliens gave the metallic voice. He said that the captive should be brought anywhere near the Chinese wall or preferably near the Himalayas. The captives should be let lose near the wall or mountain and the CARD members should clear the way for them to be picked. No attempt to trace the picking vehicle should be made. No attempt should be done to attack the captive or the crew. They should wait patiently till such time the captive reaches the flight 777 and the humans would be released. The base commander understood the entire position and started contacting through his resources, the CARD and informed the entire episode. The CARD was first hesitant to take up the news but on learning the entire episode came to a conclusion that there was possible sabotage with the flight 777 it prepared for the eventuality. The emergency meeting of the CARD was called for and the main discussion was that the four Chinese and lone Indian had been abducted along with 200 odd passengers amongst whom more of Chinese were present. The CARD members came out with lots of suggestion. The suggestions were one by one analyzed and it was decided to release the Aliens under captivity.

The CARD high command took such decision with reluctance only. The hard earned effort of holding few Aliens and doing research on them was not an easy task and once started could not be that much easily be abandoned. The enormous data collected would have to be wasted. There would not be any check mechanism to test with the Aliens. The structure of bone, tissues, cells, DNA and other details cannot be wasted. The CARD was also worried about the Chinese who were taken as hostages. Those scientists had done extensive research on Aliens and could not be just like that lost. There were repeated discussions on this point among the top leaders and it was finally decided to release the Aliens held captive by the CARD.

The CARD members prepared for the show. They went to the cell where the captive Aliens were kept under custody. They released all the gadgets that were testing the Aliens. The container in which the captives had been held amidst kerosene liquid was removed to another destination. The captive Alien shook off his body when he was brought to open and gave a big metallic roar. The entire area was echoing the sound and it looked like a terrible scene. Other than the handcuff like bondages all other hurdles for the Aliens were removed and the Aliens were loaded on to a military special helicopter to take them to a place near a isolated area by the side of the Himalayan range where they would be picked by the other Aliens. The helicopter had all the safety equipments and self defence system to face possible attack by the Aliens. All military radars were set towards the scene so that any act could be recorded for future course of action. The Aliens looked pathetic unknowing what was happening. They were curious enough to look on for their counterparts around. They were also amused the way the Chinese had been dealing them.

On reaching the spot the Chinese ordered the Aliens to get down from the vehicle. The Aliens did not understand their commands. The Chinese pulled their hand and left them at a lonely place and moved away. The information was given to CARD officials who in turn informed the commander of the base. The commander of the base started the negotiation again with the Aliens of flight 777 and informed them that the Aliens had been off loaded near the Himalayan range. The leader of the Alien team took the message and went into the cockpit and had a discussion with the other Aliens. He was of the opinion that the Chinese should be taken with them to locate the place where the Aliens had been left. There was another idea that they should not be taken to Chinese border. It was finally decided to take one of the Chinese with them to locate the place. The Aliens made arrangement for a smaller Alien vehicle to carry two of the Aliens and one Chinese with them. The vehicle resembled a UFO and darted off into air. The vehicle had excellent communication system and was receiving some coded messages from somewhere which could not be deciphered by the Chinese. The Chinese were curiously looking into the speed with which the UFO like object was flying and while flying it was surpassing many planes and moving objects which could not be identified by the Chinese. The Aliens were continuously talking in a metallic voice with someone or other. It looked as though they were taking instructions from somewhere. The Aliens had set some equipment which showed the earth view and insisted the Chinese to locate the nearest area to Himalayan border where the CARD authorities would have left the captive Aliens. The Chinese located the China wall near the Himalayan range and the Alien vehicle started rounding the area starting from a large circle and reducing the diameter to smaller one. The Alien's vehicle was reading all signals from the earth and was navigated nicely skipping all the signals with extraordinary speed. The Chinese were wondering the ongoing things. The Aliens made many rounds in that vicinity and started lowering the vehicle to locate the Aliens who had been released. The vehicle was taking all signals from the earth and the equipment inside the vessel suddenly started giving some special signals which the Chinese had not noticed earlier. The signal was picked up from the Aliens and the faces of the Aliens in the vehicle changed. They were using a telescope which looked very powerful to locate the Alien released by the CARD. After locating the Alien they gave the telescope to the Chinese and in a metallic voice ordered the Chinese to look for any force in and around the area. The Chinese looked through the powerful telescope and gave back stating that the area was free. The unsatisfied Aliens again rounded the area and suddenly in no time made a steep dive into the landscape and just stood in front of the released Aliens and in wink of an eye time they picked up the Aliens and darted upwards so quickly that the Chinese inside the vehicle was astonished with the speed and sleek act of the Aliens. The Alien's vehicle had the captive Aliens inside it and it started going up and up to escape any possible attack from the Chinese territory or from other territory. The Chinese found that the time they had taken to reach the place was much less than the time taken now to reach their flight 777. The Alien's vehicle had indeed made a roundabout route at high altitudes so that no radars or equipment could detect them. The vehicle again made lots of round before getting down. Again while getting down it made a sharp and quick darting landing and stood in front of the flight 777. The flight 777 was calm and all inside should have been fed with the available food and water. Everyone was silent inside the flight. But they were surely perplexed about the things happening around them. The Alien vehicle opened and the leader of the vehicle made some sudden checkups and pushed them back into the vehicle. The leader gave instructions to the Alien's team to take all members to the balloon and ordered them to get ready to take off. The Chinese was left in the cockpit.

The commander of the base was repeatedly calling the flight 777 through the radio. Lim was unable to give any feedback. Now that he could see the Aliens into safe custody of its leader, he approached the leader and asked his permission to talk to the base commander. The leader permitted him to talk to the base for a limited time. He said the flight could get refueled once the leader gave directions. Now it was Lim's turn to question the leader of the Aliens. He asked the leader why he had taken the Chinese captive. He argued that when they wanted to take the Aliens from human's captivity; they should also release the Chinese. The leader was visibly happy and he nodded his head favourably to the question of Lim. He called one more Alien who immediately came through the small vehicle. The two Aliens got closeted inside the cockpit. There were Lim his son Nishubdh, two Aliens – the leader and his man and the lone Chinese who had accompanied the Aliens to identify the China Wall and the Himalayan range. The other three Chinese were in the yellow balloon. The leader started congratulating Lim. He was very thankful to Lim for whatever help he had done to them. Lim asked them a pertinent question. He asked what happened to the three Chinese who had been taken to the balloon. The leader informed Lim that they would be pushed into the cockpit at the right time. He assured that, since the Aliens had been released the Chinese would also be released for sure. Then he called Nishubdh and asked him to stand straight. He and his other Alien took Nishubdh one by head and one by his shoulders. They started pressing Nishubdh. This perplexed Lim and he did not know what was happening. For a while he thought that they were crushing Nishubdh and they were trying to kill him. Lim even shouted in high pitch when Nishubdh was reeling in pain. But in no time Lim could notice lots of changes all over the body of Nishubdh. He was losing the Alien form and was slowly getting the human form. Lim was surprised to see his son so handsome and was startled to see what was happening there. In no time everything happened and Lim was extremely happy to see his son as a handsome boy. Then the Aliens came out of the cockpit and straight went to the seat of the Indian Shanthi. They talked to her in metallic voice and it was understood by her easily. They looked to thank her which she acknowledged. Lim was stunned to listen to the same metallic voice reply from Shanthi. Shanthi was replying them in their own language and thanked them also for agreeing to release all under captivity. She requested that the Chinese held captive in the balloon may be released. The Aliens accepted to her request and said that they would be released in the last minute.

It was March 22nd and the day started with the beaming Sun coming out with full beam all over the horizon. Lim got the flight fuelled, took necessary food supplements and water for all passengers. Passengers became restless that they had been sitting for quite number of days without knowing what was happening. However, everyone refreshed themselves then and there and was able to freely move here and there. Their only anxiety was to know when they would be released to their destination. Lim expressed to the leader about the final phase of the entire episode. He wanted to know when the plane could take off and when the Aliens would leave them free. The leader said that since their requirements had all been met there could not be any delay and requested Lim and Nishubdh to come to the cockpit. The leader hugged Nishubdh and handed over him a sword like thing which looked very much artistic. He handed that over to Nishubdh and said that by holding that high in air at any time in his life he could request for the help of the Aliens. Nishubdh was instructed to do so in loneliness so that he would be able to meet any of the Alien member with whom he could converse. The Chinese was restless inside the cockpit. He was asking Lim to confirm the release of the other 3 Chinese men so that he could talk to them. He was repeatedly arguing with Lim that the Aliens were not keeping their promise to him. Lim was controlling the Chinese and told him that he would somehow get the Chinese released from the custody of the Aliens. He told the Chinese that step by step everything was flowing properly and requested the Chinese to remain calm. By the time the leader of Aliens was giving the sword to Nishubdh, the lone Chinese set his eyes on the bottles with the blue liquid. When Nishubdh and Lim were moving here and there he just opened the bottles and tested it to be kerosene. By the side of the bottles he saw the spray nozzle which could be fitted with the bottle. In a fraction of a second the Chinese took the kerosene bottle and fitted it with the spray nozzle. He was expecting the right moment to spray it over the Aliens. He never had thought about the repercussion that would be left with after that event. Lim, the Alien leader and his associate along with Nishubdh went inside the flight 777 and congratulated everyone for their tolerance. Some of the passengers strangely looked at the Aliens but however thanked them for leaving them free. The team went through the plane and just reached the cockpit. The team one by one entered the cockpit. The leader was coming at the last. First Nishubdh entered followed by Lim, the associate of the Alien leader and the Alien leader. The Alien leader in fraction of second went near the exit to get into the balloon. By the time Lim moved, the Chinese who was waiting for the opportunity sprayed forcefully the kerosene in the spray bottle on the associate Alien. Within no seconds the Alien sublimed into air. There was smell of celluloid burning. In other words smell of Camphor burning was felt in the entire cockpit. The Alien leader just at the entrance magically flew and was nowhere to be seen. Both Lim and Nishubdh were perplexed and they shouted at the Chinese for his nonsense act. Nishubdh was totally taken back. In flash seconds he injected the sword into the body of the Chinese. The Chinese fell in no seconds. Lim was totally confused. He stared at Nishubdh who looked cool and said, "Dad, I never expected this bad reaction from this man and he deserved the punishment." Lim was speechless. His worry was how to account for the four Chinese. He peeped out and requested Shanthi to come into the cockpit. Everyone felt the smell of Celluloid burning and started peeping in. Quickly, Lim closed the cockpit door after taking in Shanthi. Lim narrated the entire story about the Chinese splashing kerosene and Nishubdh inserting the sword. He looked tired. Shanthi understood the situation and asked Nishubdh to hand over the sword. His hands were trembling. He apologized for his act and was shivering for his act. Shanthi put her thumb on his forehead and pressed it for quite some time. Soon Nishubdh became normal. She asked him to place the sword on the seat and started staring at the sword for quite some time. The sword started losing its shape and sublimed into air. She then moved to her seat.

While this dramatic act was happening the leader of the Aliens who exited from the cockpit door swiftly reached his balloon. He thought some nasty trick had been played by the Chinese and wanted to punish his team. Outside the aircraft the yellow balloon started drifting from its place. The drift which was very slow initially became very fast and the balloon was disappearing in no seconds. There was a metallic voice reaching the communicating equipment of the flight 777. Nishubdh immediately switched on the voice recorders and the metallic voice said like this, "The mission of the Aliens is over. The Aliens are taking the captive Aliens back to Alien state. The Aliens are not pardoning the Scientist who destroyed the innocent Alien by spraying kerosene on him. Because of this bad and ungrateful act, the Alien team is taking all the Scientists along with them. If the human race is capable of reaching the Alien state they can identify the Scientist gang and take them back. This is the prize they have to pay for ungratefulness." The metallic voice stopped abruptly. Lim, his co pilot and Nishubdh were inside the cockpit and Shanthi came back to her seat. Everyone was asking about what had happened inside. She was silent.

Lim contacted the commander and said that the hijackers had suddenly vanished. Lim also wanted permission for taking off and requested that message could be given to his country as to take which direction either the starting destination or the end destination. He was given permission to land the flight 777 at the Chinese destination as planned. It was March 22nd when the drama came to a close. The flight was given permission from the base. The commander himself had entered the cockpit and met the passengers and greeted them. He saw the Chinese lay dead and saw Lim. Lim narrated the entire story of how he carefully dealt the entire Alien team but how the Chinese had spoiled the attempt inadvertently. The flight started its journey again and was leading to the Chinese destination. The flight was received as emergency landing and all the doors and gateways were closed and special task force were guarding the airport. The flight 777 landed smoothly and all the passengers alighted. Police had entered the plane and were searching for the Chinese and Indian. They could only locate the Indian only and Chinese were found missing. They were also eyeing for the four fake passengers but in vain. Lim and his son along with the co-pilot were taken into custody by the Chinese authorities for questioning. They were along with the lone Indian taken through the special entry. There was no special check up and Shanthi was beaming with smile and leading the team with the sword in her baggage hiding from its physical figure because of the Tantric capabilities of the lady.

WHAT HAPPENED IN INDIA?

In India Mr.Kumar became suddenly famous. He was approached by many people. Politicians were thronging his residence seeking appointment. His bank friend darted into his house. He was shouting at his high pitch. "Kumar you are great". He hugged Kumar and pushed the sweet he had brought."

Guruji's Ashram woke up with bustling activities. The message of the safe landing of passengers was delivered by the ashram. There was also a sorrowful message that some damage to the passengers had taken place. The message that the lone Indian among the 5 scientists bound for conference at China was surviving and one Chinese was killed and three were abducted by the Aliens. Lim's country officials had reached China. They joined the enquiry conducted by the Chinese authorities. Everyone was spell bound when Lim was expressing the entire episode. The Chinese team enquired all the three individually and also enquired Shanthi and took her revelations on the episode. Finally it decided that the Aliens had killed one Chinese and abducted three Chinese scientists. They vowed to get them back. The flight 777 was taken back from the Chinese land with its own country official on board.

The flight 777 was gliding over the blue sky and was waiting for landing at the initial destination. Azhagi was eagerly waiting for the safe return of his son and husband. She was following the TV news channels. She was terribly happy to see Nishubdh as a young and handsome boy. The three family members got united by god's grace.

STORY 2

GOLDEN FLIGHT TO DUBAI, THE INDIAN FAMILY HAD!

Mr. Joe was working for National Bank, India. He was a dedicated Bank officer marketing all varieties of Insurance products through his Bank. He was such a lovely person that all the customers of the bank used to love and admire him for his talents and service.

In the year beginning, the Insurance Company announced some incentive scheme for the marketing officers of the Bank. The incentive scheme was that whoever sold maximum number of policies in that particular year would be facilitated with a foreign trip in the name of training. In addition to the foreign trip they would be eligible for some incentives then and there probably for the quarter ending results. The dedicated Joe went round and round and started taking policies. He could meet lots of businessmen, professionals and company executives and canvass business for the bank. The customers also responded positively and gave good business to Mr. Joe. Mr. Joe always stood on some principle. He would not take policy for the sake of taking policy cover insurance. He would go through the customer's details and plan out a programme and then sit with the customer and earnestly convince the customer about the requirement of the policy for him or his family. This approach of Mr. Joe was liked by many clients and thus business started flowing for Mr.Joe. Mr.Joe crossed the first quarter business and received Rs.10,000 as gift voucher.

That evening when Mr. Joe returned home, everyone in the family was happy to know the information. Mr. Joe's daughter was very happy and jumped saying that she would get her requirements from the voucher her father had got. Mr. Joe's wife was very happy to go out with the family. She was more thrilled to go with her daughter to get the things she wanted. She could not allocate funds for her daughter's needs for quite some time because of the spiraling prices. She was unable to save any thing for her daughter's request. This voucher came as blessing in disguise. The gift was in the form of a bank gift card. All the three entered in to a shop and bought whatever was possible. Mr. Joe's wife was telling that many more such gift cards should come to them.

Mr. Joe was not very comfortable with this scheme. Even though he was happy outwardly while receiving the presentation on a glittering evening from the hands of his Zonal Manager, his inner self was torturing him. He thought that such massive gift schemes only unscrupulously motivated many undeserving marketing officials. His concern was that many marketing officials, who were bent upon receiving such gifts, exposed the bank's customers to unknown risks. He used to argue with some of his colleagues that they should not land the customers in jeopardy by selling those policies which are not suitable to them or overselling policies by telling overstated investment returns.

Mr. Joe was a disciplined man. He always sat with the customers and really explained the policy details and made the customers to understand the policy. He used to make them understand the intricacies in the policy and first used to convince them with his clear thoughts and ideas. Only after the customer was convinced he would go ahead with arranging for the policy. The Insurance company officials also had a good rapport with Mr. Joe and they used to regard him because of his thorough understanding of the policies and creative application of his mind on selling the policies. Even the country head used to be careful with Mr.Joe when the policy details were argued amongst the officials. Similarly in the open meeting the Insurance top officials would acknowledge and say that they would not dare to show any over statements as long as Mr. Joe was in the audience. This was the regard everyone had for Mr. Joe.

Days rolled and months followed. Mr.Joe was very keen in meeting out nearly the fifty odd branches that were coming under his control. He used to even stay till night 12 o'clock at customer's place to get business. He never allowed his superior officials to chide any of the marketing officials. He was more or less the leader of the marketing officials. He used to help his fellow officials to meet their target and each and every attempt of his would be meticulous. Once in a meeting one of the superior officials chided the team saying that marketing officials never did any business and only spent their timings by sleeping in their house during business hours. The official had quoted that the marketing officials always dodged the management and skipped office and diverted their time for sleep or for doing personal work. Mr. Joe was annoyed about it and one day he took the official along with him around 10 AM and then on he took the official with him till midnight. The last client was at a hill station. The executive could not bear the chillness and he was forced to take an apology from Joe for chiding them. He later even openly praised the attempts of the marketing officials for their untiring effort to reach the target of the bank.

The year end came and on the last day of the year, Mr. Joe very hectically worked and made the entire team eligible for getting an award from the Insurance Company. Everyone in the team was happy and was pretty sure that they would get some incentive from the company. Mr. Daniel who was in-charge for Insurance Company talked to Joe and congratulated him for the team efforts and said that he would talk to his high command and arrange for a better gift to the team as such. He was appreciating the efforts of the entire team and hence he suggested a better gift for all of them. Mr. Daniel was such a nice person that he fought with the high command and arranged for a trip to Dubai for the entire team. As a surprise, he met the top official of the bank and informed him that the entire team had been given a free trip to Dubai. The top official of the bank was very happy but jealous too. However, he could not show it outside but called the team sincerely and congratulated them and handed over the intimations. The intimations contained list of items to be done by all the marketing officials for availing the benefit.

The intimation was handed over to the team in one fine evening which was conducted as a simple prize distribution function. Many branch managers envied the situation and lamented that the marketing officials were enjoying the benefit by utilizing their branch customers. Mr. Joe had in fact got gift cards for the entire branch managers during the year. But still some always lamented about this.

The team got their intimations about the trip. The letter stated that the Insurance Company was arranging a training programme at a foreign destination to motivate the bank's officials. The intimation insisted that the officials should arrange for certain credentials and submit the same to the Insurance Company. The Company would receive the credentials and after scrutiny, would make arrangements for the trip. Mr. Joe was keen in making all the people to take up the opportunity. Some had said that they would not be able to take part in the trip due to various reasons. But Mr. Joe volunteered to talk to the families and made them to accept the offer, so that the entire team could go as family group. Even though that idea did not succeed, Joe was able to convince the family members that at least the officers should be spared to go as a team.

Days moved and suddenly one day there was a communication from the Insurance Company to Mr. Joe to come and collect the necessary papers for his team's travel. The in-charge of the Insurance Company had requested Mr. Joe to take care of the entire team on behalf of them and requested that he could take the lead in arranging the tickets for the entire team. The official of Insurance Company told Mr. Joe that arrangement would be made with the airlines office to make the Visa and tickets for the entire team and Mr. Joe should go to airlines office one day to co-ordinate with them for arranging for the Visa and tickets. Mr. Joe was also happy to take up that assignment. He collected the details of all his team mates and proceeded to the airlines company. The front office of the company was excellent and the ambience of the airlines company was gorgeous. The counters were made out neatly and young smart and beautiful girls with smiling face received Mr. Joe and greeted him on the event. Mr. Joe introduced who he was and showed the letter received from the Insurance Company and from that moment, the counter lady became friendlier even. She was telling Joe that the Insurance Company had given all instructions to them for taking care of the team of Joe and assured that she would do all necessary things for arranging their visas and tickets. Mr. Joe was standing in front of the counter and after checking the letter, the counter lady who was very beautiful, insisted that Joe should occupy the chair in the waiting hall and wait for his turn. Mr. Joe was slightly perturbed about this. He thought that visas and tickets would be kept ready by the airlines office. But the counter lady had asked him to wait to get the Visas and tickets. She alternatively suggested that she would make the Visa papers and tickets and call him so that he would come and collect the tickets from her. Mr. Joe decided to wait and take the tickets. The peon at the hall very decently showed the way for his seat and Mr. Joe occupied his seat. There were colourful TV sets, filling the area. The smell coming out of the sprayer came through the AC lines which made everyone to look fresh. In addition to the television channels, there was channel music which enthralled everyone waiting in the lounge. Mr. Joe was wondering whether the government airlines office would be that much showy and comfortable. Mr. Joe was waiting for his turn to be called. He was keeping all the documents in tact so that he could just throw the documents, take the tickets and run away from the place to enjoy deep slumber at his residence. Joe was repeatedly seeing the lady official at the counter. He thought that his daughter should also one day adorn that seat and felt that she would fit in that place very suitably. He was more or less staring at her and her way of working. The excellent ticket covers and the colorful pages of the tickets all glittered in the lighting arrangement. One person who had taken the ticket came and sat by Joe's side and Joe was giving a look at the ticket. He was impressed the way tickets were issued. He was eagerly waiting for his tickets to adorn his hand.

It took some time for the tickets to land in his hand. Mr.Joe ran his hand over the smooth colorful ticket and just opened the ticket. Things were hazy but he could decipher the word Dubai and he was more or less settled that since he had directly come at the instructions of the Insurance Officials there might not be any problem in those tickets and counted all the tickets and went home. Next day he distributed all the tickets to the concerned persons. He gave clear instructions to his wife and daughter what should be done and what should not be done at Dubai. He also prepared some check lists to be completed before leaving for Dubai. Wife and daughter patiently heard all his nonsense instructions and started doing accordingly. He gave clear instructions how to use his savings in buying important things only at Dubai. He was telling his wife that Dubai was a very costly State and just like that money could not be thrown away. He cautioned that any extra items that would be taken from the hotel would attract heavy price which were other than the goods supplied by the travel agency.

Mr. Joe's wife was overwhelmed with the offer of tickets. She started talking about this to her neighbours and was discussing about the things to be purchased at Dubai. All her neighbours uniformly told her that Dubai was famous for gold. They were telling that Gold from Dubai would be pure and chains with good designs could be purchased by her to be used for the marriage of her daughter. They also said that some stylish designs could be selected for her. Some suggested some good scents and perfumes and some suggested dry fruits to be purchased. One of the neighbours suggested that diamonds were very good at Dubai.

Late in the evening when Mr. Joe had reached home, his wife came and sat by his side. She affectionately gave him the coffee she had prepared for him. Joe was wondering about her attitude but thought that she was after all taking care of a good husband. She slowly started telling about whatever she had from the neighbours and the moment she started, Mr. Joe retorted saying that she should not have talked about the trip to her neighbours. His wife was initially upset but she took control of the situation by saying that she had not told the entire story but had only just enquired about Dubai. She was saying that she talked to her neighbours referring the Dubai festival advertisement that had come on the paper. She understood the situation and postponed her discussions to night when he would also be calm and cool. Night came and Mrs. Joe found the atmosphere suitable for taking up the topic. She told Joe that she had saved quite some money by using the gift cards. Joe asked how it could be possible. She said that she purchased all the monthly requirements through the gift cards and saved the money. Joe was very happy. She stealthily dragged Joe into the topic of gold jewelry. She said that it was time for them to save some thing in gold for the sake of their daughter. Being cool Joe did not frown and thought that she was very dutiful and just listened to her. She said that she had cleared all the dues in their credit cards and some sizeable jewelry could be purchased by them in Dubai. Joe was silent.

The day of travel was fast nearing and all arrangements were being made ready. Joe and two other persons only had preferred to come with the entire family. Many had planned to come singly only. On the day of travel all of them met at one particular point at the airport and one representative officer from the Insurance Company had come to the Airport to facilitate the travellers. He had brought some sweets and snacks for the travellers along with a greeting card from his superior. Joe helped him to identify all the officers and handed over them their greetings and packets. Every one took leave from the representative officer and moved towards the counter. The tickets were checked by the officials. Joe was quick to ask for a window seat for the enjoyment of his daughter which the counter clerk obliged. From the ticket counter they shifted to the immigration counter where the officials checked their travel documents and allowed them to go to security check. Their hand baggage were checked and they were allowed inside the departure hall.

Mr. Joe's daughter was thrilled to see all the formalities and was jubilant about her maiden flight and was repeatedly talking to her mother on various things. The Call for flight departure came and all stood up and rushed to the queue. It was a pleasant experience for her to go through the passage and get into the aircraft. With a smile the air hostess received them and showed them their seat. By the time all got settled the initial formalities started and Mr. Joe's daughter took her favourite juice and some chocolates. She took the ear phone from the steward and settled for music.

The flight took off smoothly and flew over the sea. It was a delight for everyone to see the scenic beauty for quite some time. Lights were switched off and in no time landing happened and all passengers were shown the way to Arrival hall. Mr. Joe was looking for the travel agent who had booked the bulk tickets for the team. The agent with the placard identified the team and waved his hand. Mr. Joe also identified him and all were very courteously taken to the nearby hotel in Dubai. The city was fantastic. All of them were staring at the shops and buildings while travelling. The Bus reached the big hotel where they were to be stationed. The team members got down and proceeded to the reception hall of the hotel where the agent had already started discussing with the reception in-charge for accommodating the entire team. The in-charge took the necessary credentials from all the team members and handed over them the necessary room keys which were in the form of a swipe card. It was a new experience for Joe himself and all went to their rooms happily. The Travel Agent gathered all people at one place and started advising them how to use the things in the hotel rooms. He was cautioning about the extra things being used other than the one allotted for them which would be very costly and should be paid from their pocket. The travel agent also gave the travel itinerary to all the team members and asked them to be ready within two hours. All the doors of the rooms got closed and the team members started getting ready for the travel schedule. The travel agent and the bus had come in time. Some of the team members who had earlier got ready came to the hotel reception hall and were taking photos in the hall with their family members. Some had come out of the hotel and took photos of the greenery there and the buildings that were standing side by. The Bus started when all the members of the team got into it and the first point of visit was the City Mall where everything in the world was available. Mr. Joe and his family members entered in to the mall and started staring at the various show rooms and shops. Slowly, Mrs. Joe was murmuring into the ears of Joe about the gold shop which was recommended by her friend. Joe's daughter was pestering for some chocolates since her friends had compelled her to bring some. Mr. Joe wanted to fulfill her request first and they entered into a shop selling varieties of chocolates. Joe's daughter was thrilled to see the various varieties and was picking up some packets. A tall man with a big mustache was just looking at them while they were taking the chocolates. They were first startled to see him. On seeing his face it would get set in your mind. Such was his face. More so was his mustache which was typical. Joe's daughter had taken 5 packets of chocolates. Her estimate was that each would have 100 chocolates in each packet. The chocolates were glittering in excellent outer wrappers and were so attractive. Joe's daughter went to the other side of the shop and took some biscuits and some other varieties of chocolates. When the chocolate boxes and other toffee boxes had arrived the billing clerks were curiously looking at the packets by turning them on all sides. It took some time before the items could be billed. There were four men at the billing counter who were seeing the boxes curiously one by one and finally another tall man with a thick mustache allowed them to bill the boxes. The entire packets were nicely put together with a greeting card from the shop and handed over to Mr. Joe's family. They came out of the shop and started moving further. The electronic shops were astonishing. Mr. Joe entered into one of the shops and bought some electronic items. He was very particular to take one very big Toshiba TV which he felt was very cheap in that mall. He informed the official in the mall about his travel plan and that official assured to deliver them at the airport and advised them to move without any trouble.

Mr. Joe's wife was curious to get into a jewelry shop. While they were taking some ice cream in the adjoining corner of the mall, the glittering board of the jewelry shop struck the eyes of Mrs. Joe. She pulled the hands of Mr. Joe and showed him the shop by her hand sign. Mr. Joe took a look at the newest mall and acknowledged the shop and assured that they would visit the shop after finishing the ice cream. Joe's daughter was also smiling on hearing that and every one of them finished their tasty and frothy ice cream. They had never tasted such ice cream in India. When they came out of the ice cream parlor they saw another team member with his family. Immediately the male, female and children session started. Each one of them exchanged lots of ideas amongst themselves and the lady suggested that they should definitely visit the gold jewelry shop and buy something there. She quoted two reasons for getting gold from that shop. One reason was that the designs were too good and the quality could be ascertained on seeing the gold itself. The other reason was that there was a lucky draw with that shop and whoever purchases for some minimum amount would participate in a lottery lucky dip and get 1 kg of gold as first price.

On hearing the news Mr. Joe's wife made it a point to get into the shop. She was telling Joe that the gold ornaments which she would select would come to the amount of minimum purchase. She was more eager to participate in the lottery lucky dip than purchasing the gold ornaments themselves. The majority Indians are more attracted by such lucky dips. Mr. Joe was chiding his wife and ridiculed the idea that they would ever get such lucky dip. He was saying that people were getting more than 10 times of their purchases and such people's name alone would be included in the lucky dip. He was saying that the trip itself was lucky dip for him and they should be satisfied with that and expecting more would amount to greed. Joe's wife never lent her ears to his sincere illustrations. She was eager to enter into the jewelry shop.

From the time she entered the shop her eyes were attracted towards the notice boards hanging there in the shop informing about the lucky dip. She approached one of the shop attendants and asked him what should be the minimum purchase. After confirming the minimum value of purchase she started moving around the varieties. She and her daughter went bay after bay and were curiously watching all jewels. The shop attendant very patiently explained all the details of each and every ornament they had seen. Mr. Joe was so tired and bored up that he pulled up a chair nearby the entrance and started listening music from the cell phone. He hinted that mother and daughter could come to him before making payment after the selections were over. Time was passing on and the mother-daughter pair had taken some nice jewelry and came near Mr. Joe. Joe's daughter tucked the shirt of her father and Joe got up and took a look at the prices of the jewels they selected from the pro forma invoice. He decided to make the payment and asked his daughter whether she was happy with mother's choice. He also jokingly said that she should get the first prize of 1 KG of gold with her lucky hand. Her daughter chided him saying that he was discouraging them when they entered. She also said that mother and daughter alone would share the total gold. Jokingly, Joe nodded his head.

The counter at which they were making payment was a bit crowded. Many Indians had come over there on holiday trip and it took some time for Joe to reach the counter. When he reached the counter he was asking the counter official about the lucky dip and its formalities. The counter man did not bother about his bickering and simply swiped the card and threw out a pamphlet which contained all the details of the scheme. The bill was clear and self explanatory and it contained an additional slip containing a special number and a chip card. There was an instruction that the chip card should be brought to the shop while collecting any gift if any. Mrs. Joe collected all the papers very carefully and took them inside her purse and after checking with the bill whether all the items were available they moved on to the next shop. Mr. Joe was mocking at both wife and daughter about the lucky dip and after some purchases they were tired and they waited at the hall and accompanied others for lunch. The afternoon session also went on interestingly and all the team members were asked by the tour guide to get assembled near the entrance of the mall. Everyone sincerely obliged guide's call lest they should be left out by the bus. Mr. Joe and family checked all their belongings and boarded the bus. It was night by that time and the bus went inside the city showing the city landscape. It was a treat to the eyes of the travellers and they enjoyed the entire ride.

The bus reached the hotel and every one alighted with their luggage. The guide gave the next day's itinerary and went. The team members went to their respective rooms and got set for relaxing. Mr. Joe's family first fell on the cot and after sometime started rechecking their purchase. Joe's daughter was pestering him to open the chocolate packets for which he refused. She got upset and started crying. Joe's wife chided him and pacified her and permitted to open the packet. Joe said that he was bothered because everything was nicely packed and neat. If the packets were opened then it would become difficult to rearrange the items. But his wife prevailed over him and asked her daughter to open the packets. Joe's daughter again retained normalcy and opened the packet and eagerly took one chocolate and started chewing. The chocolate initially was sweet but later became bland and she removed the same from her mouth and told her father that it was not chocolate and something else was being felt. Joe was perplexed to know that. Initially he felt that he might have been cheated. He asked his daughter to spit the chocolate on his hand and held it in front of the water tap. The chocolate like thing looked like a small packet. Joe pacified his daughter and asked her to take some other biscuit and check which she obliged. There were real biscuits and the problem rested there temporarily. Joe's daughter was so tired and she fell asleep and went into a deep slumber.

Joe was tenser about the biscuit packet. He went near the water tap and took the remaining chocolate portion and looked at it curiously. He called his wife who was rearranging all the packets again. She came immediately on hearing the tense voice of her husband. Mr. Joe wanted her to take out scissors to tear open the packet like looking chocolate. When he opened the chocolate cover he was astonished to see what was inside. There was a thin container and when that was opened to his rude shock he found small diamonds inside it. His heart came to a standstill and his wife was curiously looking at him. There was fear on one side of his face and astonishment on the other side. His wife was saying that she had come across a parallel event when she was young. She and her friend had purchased some chocolates from the Burma Bazaar at Chennai, India. While opening the chocolates they found a worthy wrist watch inside it.

Mr. Joe sat down on the bed. He did not know what to do. His wife went near the door and checked whether it was locked. After deep contemplation they decided to open few more chocolates and found that every one of the packets contained diamonds. The diamonds looked precious and being a lady she could estimate them to be costly ones. The total diamonds would be hefty lottery but both were afraid about the forthcoming troubles if any. They both assimilated the message and decided to be silent on the issue. They packed everything very carefully and put them inside the new suitcase which they had purchased from the nearby shop then. The suitcase had excellent lock system and Mrs. Joe put everything inside it with a good packing of black cover over it. She positioned the packets inside the luggage and put some dress materials over it so that no one could see it apparently and come to know about anything. She did not even want to share with other members that she ever purchased chocolates from one of the shops. Both of them went late into sleep. The next day it was by 10 o' clock they had to start. Both of them went into deep slumber.

Next day morning both Mrs. & Mr. Joe woke up when the alarm continuously rang. The alarm was for getting ready for the next day's schedule. They ordered coffee for them. While they were expecting coffee, the door bell rang. Mr. Joe peeped outside expecting coffee but saw the travel agent outside. The agent entered the room shouting, "Sir! I knew you were lucky. Suddenly you have won a jackpot!" Mr. Joe was startled when the agent said that. He thought that the agent had known about the chocolate box and was blinking to give reply. Mrs. Joe was speechless. She was wondering how that agent came to know of the diamond matter. She did not want to say anything and kept silent. The agent was going ahead saying that on the previous day night itself he wanted to contact them after knowing the jackpot. This further agitated the couple and they became totally restless.

God saved them. The agent relaxed and said that he was happy to inform that they had won the lucky dip at the jewelry shop and that the authorities had tried last night itself to contact them. When they could not locate them, they had contacted the Agent to identify them and inform the result. The couple was speechless. Mr. Joe could not express himself. The agent shook him and said that they had won the 1 kg gold in the lucky dip and they would be asked to come to the shop at any time. Joe could not believe his ears. He was wondering whether whatever was happening was in reality or not. He was staring at the agent. The agent said that after that days' itinerary they could go and collect their prize from the shop. He reminded them to take the receipt and chip card that they had taken from the shop without fail. By that time Joe's daughter had woken up and she too joined the conversation. The agent congratulated her for winning the prize which she did not understand initially but later understood the same.

Shock, surprise and happiness surrounded Mr. Joe's family. They were in jubilant mood. All other team mates had come to know about the message and were congratulating the Joe's family. Some were jealous amongst them since the lucky dip prize was too worthy. The three did not know what to say and do. They mutely saw the happenings and enjoyed. Mr. Joe started murmuring something in the ears of his wife and daughter. The noise got reduced and everyone started for the day's itinerary. The agent came to the hotel in time. All at the reception were staring at Mr. Joe's family and murmuring amongst themselves. The entire scene was something new to the child. The team members made some noise at the reception hall and all the other people who had come to the hotel were staring at them. The team in entirety came out of the hotel. Some came and whispered into the ears of Mr. Joe that they would come for the prize distribution ceremony. The trip for the day ended well. There were some guests for Mr. Joe. The moment Mr. Joe entered his room, they followed him and informed him that they are from the jewelry shop and informed him the official information after checking the vouchers from Mr. Joe. The team was accompanied by some make -up artists who wanted to groom the family members for the presentation ceremony. The family accepted for the same. They dressed nicely and presented for the make-up. The team had come in a special vehicle and they took the family members and some others also to the venue for taking the lucky dip. The function was grandly arranged and the glittering function gave the family a chance to enjoy the media lights. The function went for nearly two hours with lots of snacks and drinks. Every one enjoyed the function. At the end of the event the shop officials presented the big box to Mr. Joe which he received happily and with a beaming smile. The family members and also some team members joined them and the entire area was filled with laughter and cheers. The event came to an end and the shop authorities had brought them back to the hotel.

On reaching the room, Mr. Joe became more confused. He was more worried about keeping the gold he had received. He opened the locker and tried to place the box. The box was very big since the locker was meant for some small valuables and pass ports. The couple even thought of opening the box and putting the contents inside the safe. But Mr. Joe was serious about not opening the box. He felt that all his team mates might start seeing the jewels and some chaos might take place. He finally decided to skip the next day's itinerary. They went to sleep thinking what would be the contents inside the box. The next day, when the bell rang for reminding to start for the day's tour, Mr. Joe said that he was not feeling well and was not participating in the tour. The agent came to his room and told him that he would get some medical help if needed. But Mr. Joe said that he had head ache only for which he had taken medicine and stayed away from the day's tour. Some of his team members also came to share medicine but Joe avoided the travel.

His concern was that the box might not be safe if they left them at the room just like that. However, that days' trip was not full day since they had to leave for that day's late night flight to Chennai. Mr. Joe's family stayed inside the room and started repacking the entire things. Mr. Joe took out a big plastic bag and concealed the golden dip kitty. He ordered food to his room and enjoyed the day. They were talking and talking about whatever had happened and were revisiting all events virtually. In the afternoon they had some sudden new visitors from the local press and local TV. The family entirely participated in the events and the TV lights adorned the room with the smiling daughter and wife giving poses for the TV and magazines. Everything was going so smooth and evening got set in. All the team members had by then returned and when they came to know about the press and TV coverage they came to the room and occupied their privacy and started discussing everything. They were talking that this event would be viewed in India even before they reached India. They all left the room and the travel agent came to meet all of them and he advised all to get ready for the departure. The entire team members got into their enclosures and started preparing for the return journey. The travel agent had given the time schedule for them to assemble at the lounge of the hotel. All assembled at the lounge and the luggage was brought by the waiters down. The big bus entered the hotel and all the members rushed to the bus to take the favourable position in the bus. Joe's family came out of the hotel. Mr. Joe got a sudden shock when he saw few men outside the lounge who resembled the persons whom they had seen at the chocolate shop. The big mustache showed them their identity. Their faces showed some expression which looked that they were in search of a person. Mr. Joe suddenly ducked his head and retreated into the hotel. He pulled his wife and daughter inside the hotel lounge and stayed for sometime there. He did not say anything to them and they looked perplexed. After sometime when more or less all had gone into the bus, the travel agent came peeped into the lounge. He saw Joe to hold the big box in his hand and was joking. He invited them into the bus and moved inside the hotel to check whether anyone else had to come. Mr. Joe peeped out and when he found the men had gone away he quickly pulled his wife's hand and along with his daughter darted into the bus. He pulled the screen inside the bus so that no else outside could identify them. He became very tense and his wife was tense on seeing the behavior of her husband. She asked Joe what was the problem? She asked whether Joe saw some thief like persons. Joe calmly replied to her explaining everything. He said that he saw the big mustache men at the hotel and doubted they would have understood that the packets had been wrongly delivered to this family. That was why they had come to collect or pluck the packets from them. Joe's wife said that she did not want any problem creeping and said that they would part away with the packets if any situation arose like that. Mr. Joe hesitantly accepted for the same. He could not conceal his trembling hands and he posed to look calm outwardly. Daughter was looking at them pathetically without understanding anything clearly.

The bus started and everyone enjoyed and yelled on the way on seeing the beautiful lighting arrangements and the big buildings decorated so nicely. They were all peeping out and enjoying except Mr. Joe's family. Mr. and Mrs. Joe looked silent and their daughter took a small nap as she was already tired. The bus took them through the city landscapes and reached out to the airport. On arriving at the airport the travel agent who had accompanied them got down first and he thanked all for the nice cooperation they had extended. He was advising all to check their baggage and get into the departure terminal carefully. He showed them the way where the different formalities were to be finished and took farewell from one and all. Mr. Joe's family counted their luggage and entered into the airport and proceeded to the ticket counter to check in. Mr. Joe was holding the golden box tightly on his hand and was showing the boxes to be put on luggage and the luggage to be carried in hand. He had taken a certificate from the shop as to the fact that the gold was given as a lucky dip prize. He got the hand luggage tags and attached them meticulously to all the hand bags. Then he proceeded to the immigration counter. The moment he turned he was shocked to see the same mustache men near the immigration counter. He was more or less sure that he would be losing the diamonds at any time. The mustache men also were in searching mode. Suddenly Mr. Joe handed over the golden kitty to his wife and moved away towards the toilets to escape from the eyes of the men. His wife also noticed these activities but did not show out any reaction and she walked towards the immigration counter and stood behind a big pillar in front of the counter and hid herself. She was peeping out to check whether the men had gone away. Suddenly from some quarter Mr. Joe came and took her hands and along with their daughter they reached the immigration counter. The men had moved away from there and the family became a bit relaxed not to see them. After checking the initial documents they moved on to the checking counter and came out of the other side of the metal detector.

Mr. Joe and family were waiting at the other end of the metal detector and to their surprise the boxes did not come out to the other side. Mr. Joe approached one of the securities and asked him why their baggage had not come out to the other side. The security peeped in and checked and came out. He called Mr. Joe inside and there was a special official who was sitting in front of the scan. The official was showing the scan to Mr. Joe and questioned him showing the black square packet. He wanted to know what was inside the packet. He was more or less shouting, telling that customers could not just like that pack things in dark covers since the scanners would not detect any thing inside the black covers. His voice was stern to Mr. Joe and Joe was looking pathetic. He did not open his mouth and stood as though he did not understand. The official took out a stick and put it on the computer and rounded the black box like packing and asked him what it was. Mr. Joe knew well if he blabbered anything, then everything would go wrong. He reconciled to himself and said that it was nothing but biscuits purchased for her daughter. By that time his wife and daughter peeped in and the inspecting official moved a bit and looked at them. He asked what they wanted and Joe's wife said that they were his wife and daughter. Suddenly the officials looked at the daughter and laughed. He told her that she had taken lots of biscuits with her from his country and he would take away some packets. The daughter was blinking without understanding the meaning. The official then released the baggage and asked them to take them in.

Mr. Joe was fully sweating and his blood pressure had gone up. He controlled himself and walked into the security cabin where he was personally checked by the officials. The officials had asked what that big packet was. Mr. Joe explained everything and showed the receipt and certificate given by the shop. The official gave a funny look and allowed them inside. Joe was not relieved of tension even then. There were reasons for his tension. After clearing the checks while proceeding towards the lobby he saw again the mustache men. He was very clear that they were searching for him only. He thought he would be caught at any time. If such controversy comes he would say that he had not opened the packets and they could take the packets and refund the amount. Joe had made up his mind. He thought by that he would be able to safely travel without increasing blood pressure. He walked with affirmative look and sat on the lounge. The call for passengers to board the aircraft was given. As usual all passengers had thronged the entry and wanted to enter the aircraft first. Mr. Joe looked around but did not see the mustache men and was bit relaxed. He felt that they would have searched for his family and would have left after not finding them. He also moved to the entrance and gave the tickets to the steward and proceeded to the aircraft along with his wife and daughter. He was welcomed by the air hostess and she showed his seat. Mr. Joe walked to his seat with his family and started putting the hand baggage at the cabin. While turning, he just saw the bearded and mustache men and just he ducked his head and sat down quickly. He asked her wife and daughter to sit immediately. His daughter said that the flight had not taken off and said would stand for some time. Her mother pulled her hand and made her to sit. Time was rolling. Joe had put his hand on her wife's hand and was blinking what to do. The golden box was heavy on his hand.

Mr. Joe decided to meet the destiny. He could not hold the golden box for long and decided to put it on the top cabin and to relax. While he got up he saw at the other corner and his eyes fell right on the eyes of the mustache men. The mustache men also had seen him squarely and Joe ducked his head and quickly sat down. He held the hand of his wife and remained silent. His body was shivering. Minutes later he had a feeling that someone was patting on his back and he knew it was the mustache men. His hand was shivering and he had a feeling that someone was putting his hand on his neck.

Sir, "Are you Ok. Sir Are you Ok". Suddenly Mr. Joe heard the voice of someone and woke up in shock. He was holding the arm of the chair very firmly. He darted up and stood. The Airlines office staff was perplexed. Sir, "Do you require water sir?. Why you are trembling sir? Is your health OK?. Shall I call a doctor". By that time someone came to his help and put his hand on his shoulder. Mr. Joe just managed himself and looked at the face of the airline's staff. The airline staff apologized to Mr. Joe, "Sir, very sorry! Since the computer terminals did not function properly I could not complete the task of completing the ticketing process for your team immediately. I had delayed. "Any how you have had a nap. But are you OK sir?" She again took pardon for having delayed his tickets and handed over the flight tickets of all his colleagues. Mr. Joe took all the tickets and counted them and put them in his bag. He wiped his sweat on his forehead. He laughed to himself about the dream he had. He felt that he was very avaricious. Yes! How could he get diamonds worth millions in a chocolate packet and also 1 kg of gold on lucky dip at the same time? Any how the dream he had in the airlines office was a wonderful dream. If only he had those events really, how happy he would have been.

Mr. Joe walked out of the airlines office calmly. He drove all the way to his home. He called out his wife and daughter and showed them the tickets. They were curiously seeing the tickets since it was their first air travel. Mr. Joe looked at the eyes of his daughter and there was a real glitter in her eyes. But Joe could not hide his laugh as he was thinking of his dream at the airlines office. It was indeed a Golden Flight to Dubai.